INDIGO

Tyree Campbell

Alban Lake Publishing

Indigo
Tyree Campbell

Indigo is a work of fiction. Names, characters, places, and incidents are products of the author's imagination. Any resemblance to actual events or persons, living or dead, is entirely coincidental.

Story copyrights owned by Tyree Campbell
Cover illustration by Karen Otto

First Printing
February 2020

Alban Lake Publishing
P.O. Box 141
Colo, Iowa 50056-0141 USA
e-mail: albanlake@yahoo.com

Visit www.albanlakepublishing.com for online science fiction, fantasy, horror, scifaiku, and more. Stop by our online bookstore at www.irbstore.co for novels, magazines, anthologies, and collections. Support the small, independent press and your First Amendment rights.

Also by Tyree Campbell

Nyx Series (Novels):
Nyx: Malache
Nyx: Mystere
Nyx: The Protectors
Nyx: Pangaea
Nyx: The Redoubt

Yoelin Thibbony Rescues (Novels)
The Butterfly and the Sea Dragon *
The Moth and the Flame *
*The Thursday Child**

Novels:
The Adventures of Colo Collins &
Tama Toledo in Space and Time
The Adventures of Colo Collins & Tama Toledo in Space and
Time: In Love and In Trouble
Aoife's Kiss
The Breathless Stars
The Dice of God
The Dog at the Foot of the Bed
The Dog at War
Indigo
The Quinx Effect
Thuvia, Maid of Earth
A Wolf to Guard the Door
The Woman from the Institute

Superheroine Novellas:
Bombay Sapphire 1 **
Bombay Sapphire 2 **
Bombay Sapphire 3 **
Bombay Sapphire **

Peridot 1
Peridot 2
Voyeuse 1
Voyeuse 2

Collections:
A Nice Girl Like You
(published by Khimairal, Inc)
Quantum Women *

Novellas:
Cloudburst
The Girl on the Dump
The Martian Women
Sabit the Sumerian
Sarrow

Poetry Collections
A Danger to Self and Others

SF for Younger Readers
Pyra and the Tektites 1: Aquarium in Space
Pyra (graphic novel) 1
Pyra and the Tektites 2: The Unicorn Stone
Pyra (graphic novel) 2

* published by Nomadic Delirium Press

** published by Pro Se Press

All titles are available from www.irbstore.com

For my wife, Beth, who started me on this journey. R.I.P.
...miss you, Babe...

001

Cedar Rapids, Iowa

The pale blue Nissan Murano was still parked across the street when Matthew Porter emerged from the Cedar Rapids main post office with a week's worth of mail from his box. Under the pretense of leafing through the envelopes, he tried to get a view of the driver, but the angle of the windshield in the midday summer sun made it almost opaque. Two days before, in the mall parking lot, Porter thought the driver might be a woman with short orange hair. Until today, he had not seen her again. Now the hair looked to be the same color, but he could not be certain about the gender. And the SUV was the same, three times now. The license plate was dark green, with pale numbers—definitely not Iowan.

The surveillance puzzled Porter. His darker thoughts, if known to the authorities, certainly warranted official attention, but he had divulged them to no one. He was, or ought to have been, faceless. Inside his own vehicle, an elderly gray Ford Escort, Porter mulled over the quality of the surveillance. If professional, the surveillance team did not care whether Porter knew he was being followed. More ominously, the obvious Nissan was there to hold his attention, while the real tail remained in the background to catch Porter unawares, should the order come down to take him. *They expect me to do something,* Porter realized. *But what?*

It did not occur to him to ask who "they" were.

He started the car and pulled from the parking lot onto a short side street that led to one of the city's main arteries. The Murano, after a delay of several seconds, reached the side street and turned *away* from Porter.

What the hell...

Without appearing to do so, Porter checked his rear-view and side mirrors. Whoever followed him now was beyond Porter's recognition. When the light changed, he turned onto the avenue and headed north and then east, out of the city, where he hoped the sparse traffic might enable him to identify the tail, if present at all. But nothing stood out, ahead of him or behind.

The guilty flee, thought Porter. But he hadn't done anything to be guilty of, yet.

Half a year earlier, Porter had been discharged from the United States Army after three years of active duty. Upon completion of military intelligence training, Porter had been assigned to an MI detachment in Munich, Germany, where he helped debrief some of the very last German repatriates trickling back from Russia. Fourteen months later, he was volunteered for a special assignment in Heidelberg. This consisted of taking batteries of tests, often with leads connecting his head and sometimes his chest to a monitoring system not unlike an EKG. He was not told the purpose of the tests, nor was he given any formal evaluation of his performance; he knew only that the tests and the results were classified, as was the assignment itself. He pulled no other duties. As long as he showed up on time for the tests, he was allowed to move about the city as he wished. Soon he took up with an exchange student named Nicole, and learned French. His ETS date arrived almost without his awareness of that fact. In short order he cleared post, flew back to the States, and received his discharge at Fort Devens, Massachusetts. Although he had incurred no injuries during his active duty, he was given a seventy five percent disability. He did not question this. The monthly automatic deposit from VA was more than enough to cover his few needs.

If professional, the surveillance might be related in some way to those tests. But if it was amateur...

Porter was unable to complete that thought. He did not consider himself so interesting. He leaned to one side to check his face in the rearview, as if to test that supposition. Military service had little changed him. He was leaner, having dropped a few pounds and tightened others. But the face, and the pale green eyes, still belonged to him. True, his appearance these days was rather haggard, but that was due to the nightmares. Those would end after he killed the killer.

Kill the killer.

Soon, Jesse. Soon.

Porter turned north on highway 13 and headed toward Coggon and the small country house he had inherited from his grandfather. The pale blue car had not returned to duty. Although that did not preclude others from joining in the chase, the highway made it difficult to determine who was on surveillance and who was merely traveling north.

Paranoia, thought Porter, and again cautioned himself against it. He'd been edgier the past three days, now that he knew how it could be done. How the killer could be killed. He felt more eyes on him... in the mall, at the gas station, in the library. It was possible—hell, even likely—that the presence of the pale blue car with its possible female redhead operator in his vicinity was nothing more than happenstance. Cedar Rapids was nowhere near large enough to make chance encounters unique.

Porter had first seen the vehicle three days earlier when he had stopped at a Taco Bell to pick up dinner. At the time, it had been conspicuous only by its out-of-state license plate, and he had thought nothing more of it. The next day at Lindale Mall it had passed in front of him as he backed into a parking slot, and he had caught just a glimpse of the driver: orange hair, pale face. The rear license plate confirmed the coincidence.

For two days afterwards, it did not make an appearance, as far as he could determine. But today it had followed him for at least two blocks, until he reached the post office, and had parked across the street. Had the engine been idling, or shut off? He could not recall which, now.

In the rearview Porter spotted a light-colored car closing on him in the left lane. He held his breath and lightened his foot on the accelerator. The vehicle was silver... a Buick. The driver's eyes were fixed on the road ahead as the car sped by him. I'm barking at airplanes, thought Porter, annoyed with himself.

Just past Coggon, Porter turned onto a narrow paved road and followed it for three miles to the long gravel driveway. After a pause of several minutes beside the house to watch the road, he concluded that no one had followed him this far, and pulled the car to the turn-around behind the house, parking near the back door.

The aroma of coffee greeted him just inside the doorway, the coffeemaker timer set before he had left for town. He rinsed a used mug and filled it, added a lump and a dollop, and settled onto a brown metal folding chair at the small card table in the dinette, where the window afforded him a view of the road. With the first tentative sip of coffee, his mind sighed. Reminders muttered from the dark nooks of his conscience nagged at him without effect. He ought to eat something. He needed more sleep. He might seek employment. Absently he worried his thumbnail at a dried splash of chili on the tablecloth. It was to this point his most productive activity of the day. The realization of a week ago, that with practice he might be able to take his vengeance, and with impunity, had led not to resolution but to uncertainty. He was unable to see what form the aftermath might take.

The fundaments of his great discovery had arrived piecemeal to shake Porter irregularly. One early morning he had awakened under the huge shagbark hickory tree a hundred yards behind the house. He had been dreaming of that tree, of having climbed it with Jesse during their childhood. Porter had never known himself to be somnambulant, but once he was awake, it was impossible to deny the fact of his location. Later that day he had been dozing on the couch in the front room and thinking he ought to go out for a pizza. Jingling in his hand brought him out of the haze—the car keys, which he always hung on the key rack by the back door, were in his hand, his index finger crooked through the key ring. Other incidents followed, until finally, three nights ago, he had dreamed of killing Jesse's killer. Of isolating the man from his security cordon, hustling him to a secluded location, and—on this occasion—plunging a knife into his chest again and again, the way the Roman senators had stabbed Caesar. In the morning, Porter had awakened with his fingers still closed around the handle of a butcher knife.

Porter fumbled the old leather wallet from a front

pocket of his denims and pried open the photo inserts. He kept Jesse hidden. Manorema Kulasingam, the Sri Lankan orphan girl he supported with monthly payments to *Kinderheim*, smiled at him from the top photograph, and he remembered belatedly that he had intended to send her a gift this month. Another promise neglected—for a moment he felt his heart heavy with self-disappointment. Tomorrow, he thought. I'll buy you something tomorrow, Rema. A business card from his Army days covered the back of the girl's photo. Next in line was a school portrait of his niece, taken ten years earlier. And under that...

The photo was that of a young man similar in appearance to himself, in his early twenties, standing beneath the shagbark hickory. Brown hair shorn to military specifications. Eyes pale in the photo, but they had been green like his own. Straight nose, broken twice, and Porter recalled having struck one of the blows. Sorry, Jesse. Sorry, little bro. I never meant...

Tears momentarily impaired Porter's vision, and he dried his eyes on the shoulder of his jersey. He could endure the photograph for only so long. Of its own accord his hand closed the wallet and shoved it back into his pocket.

At length Porter leaned back in the chair, hands folded at the edge of the table, dozing with his eyes open. His dream memories summoned images of the two brothers playing catch with a football, hunting for snakes in the woodpile, cribbing notes for college classes. The haunting faded with their enlistment together in the Army, with the first weeks of physical training, running uphill on the gravel road—

Porter came awake with a start, blinking rapidly. A pale car was pulling up the driveway.

The car: a light blue Nissan Murano.

It passed directly in front of his window and parked beside his Ford as if it belonged there. Porter, now on his feet, debated whether he might require a weapon, though there were no firearms in the house. Through the window in the back door he watched the driver alight from the vehicle: a slim young woman with orange hair. She approached the back door as if she meant to enter without knocking. While Porter stood frowning, she entered without knocking.

She gave Porter a moment to assess her. He reckoned her height at just under six feet, giving him a three-inch advantage. She had a short cap of hair the color of freshly-sheared copper, as stiff and unyielding as her erect carriage. She was wearing a dark green and white plaid, long-sleeved flannel shirt with the sleeves rolled up to the elbows and the tails tied loosely in front, and under that a lime green bandeau of some kind, and black denims like his own, and Army jungle boots with canvas sides and deep treads. She did not appear to be armed.

Her pale face was oval, and liberally seasoned with splotchy freckles. Thin lips pursed as she regarded him with eyes of palest silver, as if she had only just now made up her mind about something. Her right hand made a little gesture of invitation, and he realized she was wearing semi-transparent latex gloves. When he failed to respond, two tiny vertical furrows formed between her ginger eyebrows. Suddenly she grinned, and said, "Terminator."

Porter found his voice. "Huh?"

Again the redhead gestured to him. "Come with me if you want to live."

002

Suriname

The pilot flicked his cigarette to the ground and crushed it out with his boot as soon as he heard faint footsteps in the thick grass behind him. He said nothing. He heard—and felt, for he was leaning against the fuselage of the airplane—the *thump* as the porters slung the heavy shipping crate through the hatchway, followed by a tinkling of D-rings as they snapped on the parachute. He did not bother to inquire after the contents of the crate. That it likely contained contraband did not trouble him. He had flown cocaine from Calgary to Bismarck, cannabis from Guaymas to Sierra Vista. Whatever he transported for Chartreuse, his present client, it was not drugs; more probably it was an article or articles prohibited from importation. He had never attempted to open any of the containers. In the first place, he could not easily do so, for they were always code-locked. In the second, he was certain that were he to discover, surreptitiously or fortuitously, the nature of his cargo, he would be hunted down and killed.

The pilot knew when they had finished loading. He also knew, without looking over his shoulder, that one of the men had remained behind after the others had melted into the jungle. He felt no fear. The elaborate scenario of a cargo shipment to lure him to this site was unnecessary, had Chartreuse intended to terminate his employment.

The pilot waited.

"It is heavier this time."

The language the man spoke was Haitian French. The pilot preferred English or Dutch or even Taki-taki, the creole *lingua franca* here in Suriname. Still, he understood enough. "How much heavier?"

"Thirty kilos."

The pilot nodded, a gesture lost in the utter darkness. The additional weight posed no logistical problems. After some rapid and crude mental calculations, he said, "I have enough fuel in the auxiliary tanks, of course. But it will cost you.”

“Continue.”

“I think a thousand Euros is fair.”

“It will be paid.” This without hesitation.

“Yes.” But the pilot knew that the man was no longer there.

003

Bladensburg, Maryland

Lights rarely shone from the fourth unit in a row of brownstone houses in an older district of Bladensburg, Maryland, because of the perpetually drawn dark curtains. To the casual observer, the signs of habitation were few: mail delivery; the monthly meter reader; and now and then, solitary individuals leaving or departing. The same casual observer might have supposed the interior to have been divided into boarding rooms for businessmen on extended visits. To some extent, this supposition was accurate. Men—and the occasional woman dressed in business attire—did stay for days at a time in the old brownstone. But none actually lived there.

The heavy oak front door opened not to a knock but to pressure on the touchpad fixed into the right doorjamb. The pad was a sensor that read DNA in epidermal cells and compared it in milliseconds to the identities of those individuals who were authorized access. These were limited to the five men and two women of Echelon, whose names and personal data appeared on no government tables or rolls; the Homeland Security Undersecretary for Special Operations, who was equally non-existent; and the Secretary of Homeland Security, who did exist, who changed with each administration, and who was astute enough to know what and what not to tell the President.

Echelon did not exist.

It was established initially as an obscure department of the National Security Agency and tasked with discovering, developing, and deploying weapons systems that were generously described as paranormal. The tasking was based on various studies conducted at a prestigious university on the Atlantic seaboard that indicated that individuals who possessed a very rare and anomalous fragment of DNA displayed an innate potential for para-normal behavior. Such behavior included teleportation, telekinesis, and what was commonly known as mind-reading. The studies came to the attention of Homeland Security some two years after the events of 11 September 2001, and two years after HomeSec created and tasked a special division called Echelon.

Over the next two decades Echelon conducted surreptitious tests on military personnel, elementary school students, federal prisoners, and various others who could be compelled or bribed to participate in the testing. The results overall were promising for seven individuals who experienced otherwise inexplicable events, such as finding a pen in a pocket thought empty, awakening away from the location at which one had fallen asleep, and speaking with authority regarding a highly classified document. Three of these individuals were military personnel, who were ordered to undergo further testing and to receive specialized training. Although they were discharged from the military on their scheduled ETS dates, their activities and locations were closely monitored pending the development of more specific and enhanced training programs. Plans were emplaced to abduct these individuals, if necessary, and compel them to undergo this training. The other four candidates—three in elementary school and one in Fort Leavenworth—were also monitored, as they were included in Echelon contingency planning.

Well into the third decade of the 21st Century, Echelon continued not to exist, but two schools of thought developed regarding the potentialities of the paranormal. The first, promulgated by Dr. Dundas Montgomery, brooked no counter-arguments. Paranormal activity was a fact, and could under the right circumstances be controlled and applied to strategic and tactical situations around the globe. To that end, Dr. Montgomery drove Research & Development like a vehicle he had stolen, working its personnel day and night for years to find methods of certain and absolute control—methods which he considered essential to the secure application of the paranormal.

With the change in administrations at the start of the third decade, Montgomery received an unexpected request to resign his post. The effect of the request was something on the order of a mallet striking a melon, and within a day he changed from an energetic and focused man in his late fifties to a stoop-shouldered senior citizen on the verge of sixty, making his way on painful feet along the halls of Echelon. He barely left an echo. Within two months, he was dead.

Montgomery's replacement, Dr. Geneva Hartland, was a product of Yale and Duke who believed in the work but was well aware that she owed her position to the whim of the president. The need to ingratiate herself overrode all other considerations. Where her predecessor had concentrated on the potential usefulness and applications of paranormal skills, Hartland quickly realized that any individual possessing such skills was quite capable of turning them against his or her controllers. The changes she sought took a few years to implement—certain personnel had to be weeded out and replaced by those loyal to her and to the president, not to Echelon—and they had to be implemented subtly and seamlessly, to avoid alerting the Personnel Division of the Office of the Inspector General. But Hartland, a stout, graying woman with her hair drawn tight in a perpetual bun and with a spinster's mouth, had achieved her positions through political skill more than scientific expertise. She was essentially a manager, and she managed her career well, consisted with her windsock loyalties.

Not long after Hartland had established her foothold in Echelon, she received a visit from Dr. Elgin R. Goode of R&D. Tall and angular, and in his early thirties, Goode reminded Hartland of a quintessential geek, all brain and no physical prowess, although he was anything but clumsy. With better knees, he might have been picked up by the NBA. She knew his resume by heart—he had chosen paranormal investigation and analysis, and specialized in telekinetic research, mostly because there were so few experts in the field that he would rise almost inevitably to be one of the leading authorities in it.

But he was also Hartland's man, and well aware that his job and his position in the field depended on his ability to tell her what she wanted to hear—or to make it sound as if it was what she wanted to hear.

Following her into her office, he declined the offer of

coffee and waited for permission to seat himself in one of the two overstuffed chairs for visitors that stood off the back corners of her desk. When she had made herself comfortable, she indicated with a desultory gesture that he was to proceed.

Goode carefully laid a manila envelope on her desk and nudged it toward her with the knuckle of his index finger. On top of the envelope was one of the new classified document covers, this one with a luminescent coppery border and emblazoned with PARANORMAL SECRET EYES ONLY in the same color. He sat back, and ran his hand over close-cropped and tightly-curled hair, and cleared his throat. "The report you requested, Doctor," he said, his voice gravelly.

Hartland put her hands together as if in prayer, and tapped the tips of her fingers against her lips. "Why don't you summarize it for me, Elgin?"

Briefly he hesitated. There simply was no way around the conclusion at which he had arrived, but to state it almost certainly meant a reduction or even an end to his work.

"What Echelon needs to do, control-wise, probably cannot be done," he said at last. "Certainly it cannot be done, given what we know at the moment."

To his mild surprise, Hartland merely gave a little nod. "Go on."

"There are only so many ways to achieve control over someone's mind, and thereby control of his actions," Goode explained, aware that he was speaking to a manager, not a scientist. "These include drugs, and what used to be called brainwashing, and subconscious triggers, even hypnotic trances. They don't work, because they all subdue the paranormal abilities. The brain must be independent in order to function paranormally."

Hartland's hands remained in place. Her sharp blue eyes peered at him over the tops of her fingertips. "What I hear you saying is that our test subjects must believe that what they are doing is for a good cause," she said. "Without that belief, we have no way of compelling them to that cause."

Goode nodded. "Just so."

"And we have no way of preventing them from using their abilities in a counterproductive manner."

Again he nodded.

Hartland got up and went to the coffee maker, and poured herself half a cup. Turning back to him, she said, "You're concerned about the effect this will have on your tenure."

Goode decided to opt for honesty. Honesty left you vulnerable, but if you volunteered to be vulnerable, you were more likely to be kept around.

"Yes, of course," he admitted. "And I wish my results were otherwise. But absent a method of control we haven't thought of yet, I see no other conclusion to be drawn from our experiments."

"I can't very well approach the president and say that we can do this as soon as we think of something we haven't thought of yet," Hartland said, without rancor.

She moved back to the chair and sat down, smoothing her pants. Goode was appreciative of the fact that she had not chosen to wear a skirt and nylons today. Her thighs made a joke of nylons. Whenever she walked swiftly down the hallways, she sounded like a steam locomotive.

Goode's face creased slightly with an incipient smile as he thought of this. It improved his mood, until he noticed that Hartland was looking at him curiously.

"You had a thought, Elgin?" she asked.

"If only I did, Dr. Hartland. If only I did."

She tapped the manila envelope with a pencil. "Very well. I'll read this, and take it under advisement."

Dismissed, Goode turned and left.

When he had closed the door behind him, Hartland took out a scrambled and encrypted smart phone and touched the pad. Within two seconds she heard the right voice in response.

"Adrian, the report I've received from R&D confirms my suspicions," she said. "I gather you still have the top three candidates under close surveillance?"

"Need you ask, Director?"

"I suppose not," said Hartland. "Very well. Regarding Anastasia Louise Somerville, Carlos Renaldo Vega, and Matthew Thomas Porter, the Command level is raised to

Action, the Authorization code is Commit. Report each resolution as soon as it occurs."

"Understood."

Black silence followed. Hartland put the smart phone away and began planning her resume for her next position. Just in case.

004

Central Iowa

Porter ignored the offer of the woman's hand. "I'll pass, thanks," he demurred. "Besides, you aren't from the future."

The woman tilted her head in birdlike fashion, eyeing him as if he were a grub that had just popped into view. The predatory expression disquieted Porter, but the moment passed as quickly as her urchin's grin appeared. In the morning light through the dinette window her eyes seemed softer now, the metallic glow gone from them and replaced by a depth of gray. Behind their blend of warmth and mirth hovered a sparkling intellect. Suddenly Porter felt as if he could peer into those eyes forever, or fall into them. He shook himself violently, a dog just liberated from the bath.

The woman frowned again. Her hand moved, started to touch him, stopped halfway.

"Who are you?" asked Porter.

"Kerise Renaud. We don't have much time, Matt."

She spoke with the faintest hint of French accent, as if English had been her primary language since childhood.

He refused to budge. "Before what?"

"I'll explain on the way." She dragged at his arm, and now her eyes entreated him. "We'll take my car. *Please*, Matt."

"What's wrong with my car?"

Matt recognized that his question signaled his surrender, and allowed Renaud to usher him toward the back door.

"Yours has a GPS locator," she said.

The objection stumped him. "Every car has one."

"I had the one in mine removed."

"Isn't that illegal?"

"Hang about." She stopped him at the door and peered through the windows alongside. Her car was parked beside his in the driveway, but she was focused further away. "Trail of dust," she told him, pointing toward the low trees half a mile away. "*Merde!*"

"Someone's coming for me?"

"You better believe it, bucko. You're a major threat to national security." She opened the door and gave him a firm push outside. "Into the back seat and get down out of sight. We'll do this the hard way."

Matt staggered against her car. "What does that mean?"

Kerise opened the back door and levered him into the vehicle. Within scant seconds she had climbed in, turned the ignition, set the 4WD, and taken off for the woods.

"There's no road in there," Matt pointed out.

"True; and they're driving a Buick," said Kerise. "Hang onto something back there. And keep your head down!"

"You're as bossy as my drill sergeant, you know that?"

Kerise glanced over her shoulder and yelled over the pounding of the car. "But your drill sergeant won't go to bed with you."

"*What?*"

"Hey, you're the one who fed me the straight line."

The vehicle swerved and braked, throwing Matt against the door and then into the well between the front and back seats. Two tires momentarily lost traction as she accelerated. "Tree root!" yelled Kerise, and Matt barely had time to cling to the back seat cushion before the left front of the vehicle flew up. The impact sent him into the back seat. Kerise yanked the wheel right and spared them a second bump. Supple branches lashed at the vehicle, and scoured the paint and windows. They drove across a corn field left fallow that year, the mound of each row jostling the car. They lurched over a berm at the edge of the field and then sped across a lawn—David Cooke's lawn, Matt guessed, given the direction they were traveling, and he half-expected Cooke's wife to charge out of the house, brandishing a broom at them. Matt doubted that Kerise was the sort of young woman one could easily shoo.

Suddenly Matt broke into a cold sweat. Who *was* she? Kerise Renaud, she'd said, the name drawing a blank. Yet her attitude and tone of voice suggested that there was something to be recognized in the name, or perhaps behind it. Moreover, she certainly seemed to know *him*—had been following him for several days. As for his being a threat to national security, as much was true—but how could she have known that? None but he knew.

How the *hell* could she have known that?

Who is she? Why did I choose to come with her?

The song of the tires told him that Kerise had found a paved road. He reckoned they were headed west for Troy Mills. He doubted the small town would improve their circumstances.

Something clanged into the rear hatch of the Murano, punching a hole in the metal. A bullet, Matt realized immediately, though he had heard no report. Kerise muttered something in French. Off to his right, Matt caught a glimpse of movement, and turned to see a Predator drone hovering. From the front a barrel projected, aimed roughly at them. The Predator slowly spun in the air, following them along the road.

"Kerise?" said Matt, unable to control the nervous tremor in his voice.

"I see it, I see it." She began to alternate between braking and accelerating to throw off the drone's aim. The drone now began to move parallel to them, some fifty feet above the cornfields.

Matt's eyes narrowed. "You weren't counting on this."

Her face grew somber. "I thought I had enough lead on them," she told him. "Commo on. Teague, tell me you're listening."

"Teague," said Matt.

She indicated a voice-activated transceiver on the dashboard. "I was taking you to the McDonald's at the Urbana exit off I-380. He was going to meet us there. No answer," she added, growling her annoyance. "Teague does... odd jobs for us."

"Us."

She swung the wheel abruptly to the left, crossing the center line, then brought the SUV back and onto the shoulder. "They're behind us now. There's an Army .45 automatic in the glove box. A clip is already in it... and don't look at me like that. You *did* qualify with one in the Army."

"Qualify, yes," said Matt, no longer wondering how she knew details of his background. "Hit anything, not really."

The drone sped on ahead of them and prepared to land, and Kerise braked again. "This is it. I'm sorry, Matt, but I can't fire accurately while I'm driving. You'll have to do it. Aim for the camera port, dead-center. If you can shatter the glass, it may ruin their vision, and buy us some more time to reach Teague."

"No way," objected Matt. "That shot is impossible."

He sat back, his head against the rest, and closed his eyes. In the quiet space, events had become an avalanche. Surveillance, the girl, the pursuit, all tumbled downhill, taking him with it. He still had no idea who Kerise was, who those chasing him were. One side wanted him dead, the other alive. But who was who? He had no time for either of them. He had a promise to keep.

He glanced at the girl. *You can't just leave her in the lurch,* he told himself. *Whoever she is, she means well.*

"Change of plan, then," he mumbled. His thoughts expanded to encompass not just himself, but the Murano and its contents. It was huge and forbidding.

Can I do this?

You have *to.*

The massive image of the Murano lumbered in his mind like some prehistoric beast, but he held it in place while he recalled the details of a prior visit to the Urbana McDonald's. A clear picture of the parking lot and the gas station next door came into focus for him. The Murano almost blotted it out, but he managed to retain both images simultaneously, and hold them fast.

"Close your eyes," he said, without opening his to look at her.

"What? *Why?*"

"It's better if you close your eyes. Do it now. And come to a stop."

"What are you—"

"*Please,* Kerise."

"This better be good."

Tires fairly shrieked on the pavement as the Murano came to a stop. Almost immediately Matt felt weightless, as if an elevator had begun its descent too quickly. A beat later, he regained 188 pounds, and his stomach lurched. When he opened his eyes, he saw through the Murano's windshield the drive-up menu for McDonald's.

"*Mon Dieu!*" breathed Kerise.

005

Munich, Germany

Langford felt uncomfortable at zoos. A native New Yorker on what he considered to be a relatively dull freelance assignment, he was standing alone near the flamingoes at the main entrance to the Munich *Tiergarten*. Peacocks wandered by, paying him no mind. But he was drawing stares from passing Germans, even though his trousers had been tailored to fall almost to his heels, in the European style. The attention assaulted his attempt at anonymity. He wondered whether one of the passers-by was supposed to meet with him, and was now verifying that he had come alone as instructed.

You will be recognized, she had said.

Because no matter what I do, I still stand out as foreign, he thought.

Once more Langford checked his Palmetto: 13:04. She was late. He continued to watch for a signal, a wave of greeting, a motion for him to approach. A blonde girl of no remarkable appearance, passing her ticket to the gateman, glanced momentarily in his direction, but she gave him no encouragement. Somewhere within the zoo, an elephant trumpeted, while Langford reviewed the instructions he had received and the manner in which he had received them. The call on the commo app had arrived without identification, and had lasted perhaps thirty seconds. Had there been an accent? No; well, yes, but very slight and definitely not German. French possibly. Age youngish, perhaps in her twenties, but Langford knew a grandmother who did the voice-over for a little girl in a cartoon. Had there been a hint of danger or urgency? Insistence, but she did not sound like a terrorist. What did a terrorist sound like? The girl next door? In Dearborn, perhaps. Affiliated and unaffiliated reporters were targeted by various groups, all clamoring for attention to their causes and agendas. She had told him to come alone. She had not forbade him to leave a note on InterBook.

Langford stiffened when she spoke. "If you turn around, you are dead that instant."

He froze in mid-turn, the Palmetto still activated in his right hand. He curled his fingers around it, to conceal as much of it as possible except the tiny monitor. A fingertip discreetly ticked Record.

"Continue watching the entrance," she went on, "as if you are expecting someone. On the hill beyond the entrance is a man with a silenced rifle. He has his instructions; if you follow yours, you will not be harmed."

"Who are you?" Get the facts first. Who, what, where, when, why, how, huh? His eyes automatically went to the hill, where dense shrubbery concealed most of the cars parked on the street there, but he saw only pedestrians on their way downhill toward the zoo entrance.

Langford sensed that she had moved. "I'm the person who has just now placed a small padded manila envelope against the low wall next to your right leg," she answered easily. "Listen to me very carefully. You are to disclose the contents of the flash drive within, verbatim and without embellishment, to the news services no earlier than August 27 of this year. Do you understand what I have said up to this point?"

"No."

She gave a little sigh of impatience. "Do you understand the instructions I've given you so far?"

"So far, but—"

"If you disclose any part of the contents of this drive to anyone at any time before August 27, you will die."

"Now wait just a—"

"*Don't* turn around." Her voice was a breath of frosted steel. "And be silent. This is not a negotiation, nor is it an interview."

Langford started. It had just occurred to him that she wished to remain unseen by him because there was a possibility that he might recognize her. Face still aimed at the zoo entrance, he strained his eyes to the side to catch a glimpse of her, an article of clothing, a shoe, anything, but he was badly positioned even for shadows, with the sun just trickling toward the west, away from him. He caught a glimpse of a pale, bare arm just before her fist rapped him on the point of his left shoulder.

"Eyes straight ahead," she hissed.

Langford wanted to rub the injured shoulder, but held still. "I'm a reporter," he protested. "I'm curious."

She did not respond. Gradually Langford twisted his right hand until the Palmetto was aimed behind him. Still he received no reaction from her.

"Can I at least buy a vowel?" he asked.

Silence answered him. He took a tentative step backward, anticipating contact, but she had moved. Another step brought him to the retaining wall against which the manila envelope rested. Cautiously Langford turned around, and found himself alone.

006

Central Iowa

Echelon Mobile Unit 17, consisting of two men in a white Ford F-350 with a camper shell, sat parked on the shoulder of the south on-ramp at Exit 49, Interstate 380, in central Iowa. Although the vehicle's A/C worked, the men had rolled down their windows. The passenger, a former Air Force captain and the older of the two, finally closed his mouth after watching the replay of the disappearance of the Nissan Murano on the remote drone monitor. A few hyphenated epithets escaped him as he glanced at his partner.

"Maybe it's something they snuck into our coffee at McDonald's," he said sourly, his Texas accent sneaking in over his Academy diction.

The driver, an Air Force tech sergeant on extended temporary duty, hesitated, then shrugged. "It can't be a glitch in the drone, sir," he noted. "We just did a diagnostic when we powered her up."

The captain grimaced. Adair always referred to drones as female, as if that made them more compliant. "There's no need to 'sir' when we're alone, Tommy," he said, for the umpteenth time. "Jorge will do just fine. Failing that, a simple Lopez will suffice." He made another face at the monitor. He knew he was talking too much, because he was just as flabbergasted as Adair. What they had just witnessed was not possible. Worse, he had to call it in, and expected an incredulous response at the very least. More likely, recriminations were in order, along with aspersions regarding the EMU team's competence.

"It's hot," said Adair. He undid his seat belt, and shed his suit coat, leaving it folded along the back window. Already his left hand, exposed to the sun as he drove, had begun to redden. The fine blond hairs on the back of it did nothing to shield him.

Lopez's fist thumped the dashboard. "*How* can an SUV just *vanish*?" he wanted to know.

"And whose was it?" Adair threw in. "That definitely was not Porter's old Ford."

Lopez played back the drone's recording. "There," he said, jabbing a finger at the monitor. "Female. Young, looks tall, short red hair. But who the fuck is she?" He struck more keys, zoomed, and isolated a side view of the woman's head, the best he had. A command sent the image to the Rec Room for identification.

Adair gestured at the monitor. "Maybe the vehicle's still there, sir," he allowed. "Could be a cloaking device."

The officer gave him a hard look, then softened just a little. "If we hadn't seen this with our own eyes, I'd dress you down for that remark, Tech Sergeant," he scolded, only half-seriously. "However, given what we witnessed, maybe that cloaking device idea isn't far off."

He set a dial and keyed in a command. The view in the monitor shifted to allow a hundred-eighty panorama six meters above the roadway. Another command enabled sensors and radar.

Lopez shook his head. "Negative. There's nothing there."

"We hope."

He sighed. "Yeah. We hope. All right, let's send it south to sweep the highway. Maybe they're nearby. Meanwhile, I'll," he sighed again, "raise D.C."

Lopez scrambled the Palmetto and got the head office in Bladensburg. He was somewhat surprised when Doctor Hartland answered; he had been expecting General Tosk, the Chief of Operations. For just a moment after her curt "Hartland," his voice faltered. But he quickly recovered, giving her the barest details.

When he had completed his report, silence followed, one he dared not interrupt. To his chagrin, his heart began to beat faster, and the sheen of perspiration thickened on his forehead and in his close-cropped salt-and-pepper hair. Hartland herself was not deadly; her orders, however, could be lethal.

"This is disappointing," she said at last.

Lopez blinked. "You did hear me say the vehicle simply vanished," he replied, with as much courage as he dared muster. "One second it was there, and the next second—"

"What I'm hearing, Jorge, is that you lost the target," said Hartland, with taut gentleness.

Lopez fought against the urge to defend himself. He noted with dismay that Hartland failed to acknowledge his statement that Porter'd had help. "We're trying to relocate it now, Director."

"Perhaps I should dispatch another EMU team to assist you," she said sweetly. "Now, you did understand the Commit order?"

"Yes, Director."

Lopez did not answer. A vehicle was about to pass by them. In the rearview mirror, the driver appeared to be completely bald, even to his eyebrows. It was a face that stood out from the dossiers in the Recognition Room that EMU personnel had to review periodically.

"Richard Hodges," he whispered, as the vehicle, a late model green Dodge, passed by. The driver did not look at them as he seemed to flick a small object through the passenger window.

"What was that?" demanded Hartland.

Lopez cleared his throat, and swallowed. "I just saw Richard Hodges," he croaked. "Or someone who looks very much like him."

"And who is that?"

The question shocked Lopez. The Director of Echelon *did not know?*

"He's—he used to be Langley, very hush-hush," he replied. "Blacker than Black Ops. He's independent now, and off the grid unless he wants on. His dossier is in the Rec Room."

"You seem to attach some significance to his appearance in the area."

"There are no coincidences, Director."

"Yes, I've heard that before. I suggest you get busy, Jorge."

She rang off before he could respond.

Adair looked visibly shaken. "What... *who?*"

"Need to know," muttered Lopez.

"If Hodges is going to be a problem, then I need to know," Adair shot back. "If I see him again, what do I do?"

"Shoot him center mass, repeatedly," replied Lopez.

"Then put one through the back of his head. Just make sure it's him." He glanced down at the drone monitor. Keyed commands raised the drone's altitude to a hundred yards, and sent it northwest along I-380.

A small *whoomp* under the pickup startled them. They flung doors open and dived away, sidearms drawn. Lopez spotted no one lurking about. Under the vehicle, the oil pan was pouring the last of its contents through a two-inch hole onto the gravel.

007

Central Iowa

"Hungry?" asked Kerise.

She had all but recovered from the shock of the teleportation of herself, Porter, and the SUV to the Urbana Exit McDonald's. The vehicle's motor was still running, and in gear, immobilized only by her foot on the brake. Porter, now in the passenger seat, was unresponsive. He seemed to be exhausted by the event, and was taking slow shallow breaths, his half-lidded eyes staring a million miles away. He did not appear to have heard her query.

"Neither am I," she said, and pulled the Murano into an angled slot.

Porter turned in his seat to face her, to confront her. "Who," he demanded, "*are* you?"

She met his angry eyes evenly. "I told you: Kerise Renaud."

He sputtered. "Yeah, you said, but... I mean, who are you? I don't know you; I've never seen you before in my life."

"And yet you got into the car with me," she said, and smiled. Her hand twitched—an involuntary response to touch his arm for reassurance. "As for who I am... it's complicated, Matt," she said.

"I'll bet," he growled. "And that drone was trying to kill us. Why?"

"Kill you, in fact," she amended. "The order went out yesterday."

"The order? *What* order?"

"It's, well..."

"Complicated. Right."

He started to get out of the car, but she locked all the doors.

"But it is," she said quietly. "Right now we need to transfer vehicles. That's where Teague comes in."

Even as she spoke, a green Dodge pulled into the slot alongside Kerise. The driver and sole occupant was a middle-aged man completely bald down to the eyesbrows. He reminded Matt of a grouchy Mr. Clean. He was wearing a green pocket tee shirt that was taut over his shoulders and upper arms. He had a hard look for Kerise as he motioned for her to roll down her window. When she had done so, he said, "They had a drone out for you."

"We know," she replied. "We managed to evade it. What's the plan?"

"There's an EMU team parked on an on-ramp about ten miles north of here. I've disabled it, but not the drone." He pointed toward a white sedan parked next to the dumpster in the back of the lot. "There's no camera coverage back there," he went on. "We need to drive over, get in, and get out of here."

Without waiting for a response, he backed out. Kerise followed, while Porter grumbled. His attitude disappointed her. There were aspects of a personality one did not get a good sense of from a dossier, including his complaints. It should have been clear to him that she was trying to rescue him, to save his life. Because of the drone, the attempt had gone slightly awry, but she was gratified to learn that Porter's psychokinetic abilities were already well-developed. Still, fear and desperation had provided the impetus for this teleportation. She needed him to control his abilities, not act on his emotions.

His accusation burst into her thoughts. "You knew something like this was going to happen," he said.

She gave him a sidelong glance. "Yes. We did," she admitted. "We had certain contingencies in place; this was one of them. I had hoped to take a simple route from your house, but that car arrived sooner than we'd anticipated. So we took the back way out. They were watching for us, and acquired us..."

She stopped the SUV. Teague was climbing into the driver's seat of the white sedan. "Stay low, and get in the back seat. I want you able to duck down if necessary." She leaned across him for the .45 automatic, and stuck it under her belt, tugging her shirt down over it. "Ready?"

"No."

She took a breath and puffed it out. Teague had already turned the ignition of the sedan—a older model

Toyota, she saw. His animated gestures indicated that time was short. She gave Porter her best earnest look.

"We're going to the Eastern Iowa Airport just south of Cedar Rapids," she told him. "Once we are in the air, I will answer any questions you have, and some you haven't thought to ask." She touched his arm. "Matt, I promise you this. Up till now we've been too rushed for explanations, but you will have them, I swear to you."

He hesitated. "Once we're in the air, you said. Where are we going?"

"Roswell, New Mexico. With a stop near Wichita for refueling."

"I have things at home..."

Kerise shook her head sadly. "Right now, your home is being ransacked—"

The Toyota's horn sounded, just half a note.

"Please, Matt," said Kerise.

He kept low, and slipped into the back seat. A second later, Kerise nudged him to make more room for herself. Unhurried now, Teague pulled the vehicle from the parking lot and onto the Interstate, heading south. She allowed herself to feel a small measure of relief.

008

Munich, Germany

Back in his hotel room, Evan Langford sat staring at the flash drive next to the Hewlitt-Packard laptop on the writing table before him. In the past, he had received all sorts of news tips from all kinds of people. Most of them were willing to provide information as long as they could give it without attribution. *Unnamed sources stated. Not authorized to speak with. Conditions of anonymity.* But none of that information had been accompanied by death threats.

Until now.

Langford's attention shifted to his Palmetto. How much of the encounter had he managed to record? On the tram back to his hotel, he had fought back the urge to check it out, fearing that someone else might see it. Now, alone, he continued to hesitate. The feeling persisted that he might recognize the girl. Worse, that should he identify her, he just might be signing his own death warrant.

And what was the significance of August 27th? He summoned the courage to activate the Palmetto's calendar. The date was a Friday. A slow news day, the day when governments released information they had to release but did not want a lot of attention paid to it. A search of historical events for that day turned up nothing that seemed relevant—a volcanic explosion, a pitching duel, a Persian defeat in ancient Greece. The act of touching the Palmetto overcame his reticence. He played the recording.

A solid view of his left shoulder appeared, and above that a cap of tangerine hair slightly tousled by the breeze. She was tall, then, probably close to six feet. Freckled forehead. Pale eyes that might have been gray. Straight nose. More freckles on the cheeks. Thin lips moving as she spoke—he had the sound muted. That was the extent of the video, but it was enough.

He'd seen that face before. Somewhere.

On speed-dial he had the number of a connection at Interpol. He tocked it.

⸻

Bladensburg, Maryland

Although not usually a peripatetic thinker, Geneva Hartland was wandering around in her office, mulling over possibilities. The wet orders had already been given regarding Somerville, Porter, and Vega. Not that she regretted them—she was incapable of that, a requisite for her office. But she was having second thoughts. The three were still assets, even if at this time they could not be controlled satisfactorily. If they were to be captured, and tranquilized or disoriented so that they could not bring their unique talents to bear, they might be celled indefinitely.

Briefly she wondered whether the trio was telepathically interlocked. It would not have surprised her. But did it in fact matter? She was not certain, and she doubted anyone could have told her. It was something to bear in mind, but it was not a deterrent to the renditions she was considering.

The disappearance of Matthew Porter nagged at her. She'd finished reading the redacted dossier of Richard Mellon Hodges, and wondered how much of it was accurate, and how much assumed. Multi-faceted and well-trained, Hodges had been the CIA's best black ops agent and now was one of the country's worst adversaries, if not *the* worst. He was capable of any act, and had proven this on too many occasions to count. It did not appear that he hated the United States, so much as he hated its enemies, and was willing to step way out of bounds to deal with those enemies. Specifically, with those who were behind the destruction of the World Trade Center. And those individuals had not—had never—been to Afghanistan.

Hodges' association with Porter was another matter, one not yet considered in his dossier. What could possibly connect him with the telekine, as she had come to label Porter? On the surface, it made no sense. She answered to but one person. The question, then: was it prudent to call the President and request Hodges' unredacted file?

At length Hartland paused and sighed. She had come to a stop at her desk. The secure phone lay directly under her outstretched hand. She scrambled it, and raised Adrian Dunbar, and issued amended instructions regarding the trio of potential telekines. Following that, she sent for the Director of Echelon Security.

***

Central Iowa

For the fifteen minutes they spent at Eastern Iowa Airport just south of Cedar Rapids, Matt kept glancing over his shoulders. Even when Kerise admonished him to relax, his eyes flicked from side to side. Sipping a soda through a straw failed to calm his nerves. With no shade available, the drink helped, until the sun warmed it. The temperature on the message board read ninety-eight, a record for that day; Porter believed it. Despite his skepticism of global climate change, he had to admit something was awry. But it could not concern him; he had other aims in mind, other plans.

Teague led the way toward the two-engine Cessna, its jets already warming. Auxiliary tanks on each wing suggested a long flight, and Porter wondered whether they would indeed stop near Wichita, or were in fact bound directly for Roswell. He was unable to make out the pilot. The airplane itself seemed to be an older model that had known wear and tear. Matt had flown in a C-130 Hercules and a C-123 while in the Army, and a Boeing 737 to and from Rhein-Main Air Base in Germany, a remote staging area for the Middle East. He had no experience in small planes. This added to his tension, until he felt Kerise's hand on his arm.

"You are in no danger, Matt," she said, her voice just audible above the noise of an airliner taking off. "Please, relax. We're almost to the plane."

"I just wish I knew what was going on."

"You will."

"Whose plane is this?"

"Mine," she replied. "Well, the pilot's, technically. But

I'm the one who decides where it's going to go, and I'm the one who pays the bills."

"And Teague?"

"He's... on loan." Matt's face twisted with questions, and she shook her head at him.

After a brief silence, he asked, "What was that remark about my drill sergeant?"

Kerise flashed a smile. "You remember that, eh?"

"It was... well..."

"Forward? That's my European upbringing. The sex is pretty much the same—I guess—but there's less guilt or shame attached to it. Your country still has a Calvinist streak that has yet to allow you lot to come to grips with your own sexuality. So to speak."

"My country," repeated Matt. "What's yours, then?"

They paused at the lowered steps that led up into the fuselage.

"*Je suis française*," she told him. "Born in Martinique, raised in French Guiana and Paris, educated at the Sorbonne and Oxford." She nudged him onto the lowest step. "You can have the rest after we're airborne."

⁂

Despite the assurance of divulged details, Matt found himself sitting alone after the Cessna left the airport, Kerise apparently having other matters that required her attention. One of these, he noticed, involved a ten-minute call on her Palmetto. He shrugged, and settled back in the seat, trying to relax. His thoughts drifted to one of the three children he supported through *Kinderheim*, a German endeavor to feed and educate impoverished children, on the same order as other such organizations except that in this instance no religion was involved. He had done some checking; almost ninety percent of the donations to *Kinderheim* went directly to benefit the children, not to some administrator's Lexus payments.

One of those children was Manorema Kulasingham, a Tamil teenager whose passion was traditional dance. She wrote some English, and they exchanged simple letters, his inquiring after her health and schooling, hers expressing gratitude for the food and other items she received through *Kinderheim.* He thought of Rema—as she called and signed herself—as his good deed. Somewhere along the line, he had decided to try to do some good, and this seemed the best way. Rema and the other two children gave him balance, tipping his scales in their direction, as against the rage he felt over the death of his kid brother.

Matt tugged his wallet free and probed into the photo compartment, withdrawing the two-by-three black-and-white photo of Rema in traditional dress, her hands and arms caught in a dance movement. She was smiling, and he could tell it was not perfunctory for an audience, but because she was genuinely happy. He hoped he had done something to help make her so.

He was about to tuck the photo back into the wallet when Kerise said, "Manorema. I'm sorry, Matt. They'll seize the letter she sent you, as well as the others you've kept."

Matt swore, softly but with hyphenated improvisation. "Is there *anything* you don't know about me?" he demanded.

"Quite a bit," she replied, taking the seat next to his. "Frex, do you want the toilet paper to unroll from the outside or the wall side?"

Matt sputtered. Gradually it occurred to him that he had no preference. Sometimes out, sometimes in. He knew it mattered to some people, but he could not figure out how it applied to his present circumstances.

Something she had said at their initial encounter sparked his mind once more. It stuck in his mind not for the promise but for the sense of outré it posed. "You did say sleep with," he reminded her.

Kerise laughed brightly. "I didn't actually have sleep in mind."

Matt turned to look out the window. The girl was impossible.

She was impossible, and so was a flight to Roswell in a Cessna to escape from people who for reasons as yet undisclosed wanted to kill him.

She was impossible, and yet he did not doubt her sincerity. But *why* would she...

"Kerise?"

"You have much to learn, grasshopper."

"I'm beginning to see that," Matt agreed. His tone took on the edge of a complaint. "Kerise, what *is* it with you? Do you have a dossier on me or something?"

"*Biensûr*," she answered. "Of course. It's even more extensive than the one at Echelon." Involuntarily his face twisted in a sudden question, and she added, "The people who are trying to kill you, Matt."

009

Roswell, New Mexico

The city of Roswell, New Mexico, was known for one thing, and one thing only. Without tourism, Roswell would be just another spot for watering horses while on the way to somewhere else. Stores sold all sorts of memorabilia, from genuine fragments of metal found at the scene to inflatable little gray women for men with a bit of kink. In many ways, it was an ideal place for two Echelon agents to blend in; nobody paid any attention to out-of-state license plates, and if Landon and Willis had already acquired sunburns on their left and right forearms, respectively, no one was likely to remark on it, except perhaps to sniff, "Tourists."

Both men had shed their suit coats to accommodate the heat, albeit with little effect, as they continued to perspire. Landon had also loosened his necktie; Willis was wearing a black bolo cinched together with a clip attached to a large replica of an Indian-head nickel. Both sipped coffee from paper cups in the drink tray on the console between them.

"Shoulda gotten water," said Willis, draining his own cup.

They had parked half a block from a one-story, flat-roof house lathered in pastel blue adobe. A couple of shade trees guarded the sidewalk that led to the front door. A few well-tended flowers in small terra cotta pots added color here and there. The garage door stood open, the garage empty. Anastasia Louise Somerville had gone some-where—in town, else why not close the garage door—and would be back soon.

The police scanner in the dashboard sizzled for a second, and the dispatcher sent Animal Control to an address in the suburbs to investigate a dog bite.

"What time is it?" asked Willis, who owned a watch and a Palmetto and could clearly see the dashboard.

"Quarter past three," Landon replied patiently.

"Maybe she went to see a movie."

Landon shook his head. "Too long. She stepped out because she ran out of milk, or something."

"It's been an hour," Willis pointed out.

"Quit worrying."

"I don't like it, Elly."

"For the last time, it's Elliott."

"I still don't like it."

⁂

The Cessna landed at Roswell International Air Center late in the afternoon. Sunlight glared through the starboard windows of the fuselage, and Matt had to shade his eyes when the airplane turned around at the end of the runway. They had just rolled past The Boneyard, where obsolete aircraft rested, parked in echelon for their retirement. He saw phalanxes of Boeing 757s and McDonnell-Douglas MD-80s. Kerise had told him that some of the older airplanes docked here were cannibalized for parts, while others constituted a museum of sorts, open for visitors.

She had not told him anything useful during the flight. She had not given him "the rest" of the story after they had gotten airborne. There were a few remarks about Mount Pelee, the volcano that had formed Martinique, and her flyover of it during an eruption. She mentioned traveling a lot: Brazil, Suriname, French Guiana, Germany, Thailand... and France, of course.

"I grew up there near Paris," she told him, that and nothing more.

For a moment when she brought up the topic of Roswell, the notion of UFOs and aliens flashed through his mind. Given what he had endured the past few hours, nothing of that nature would have surprised him. Still, she looked human. Very much so.

"Why Roswell?" he asked—for the tenth time—after the Cessna taxied to a halt near what he assumed was the Air Terminal.

Instead of answering, she motioned to Teague. He got up, opened the hatch, and extruded the steps. More sunlight bathed Matt, blocked only momentarily as the

37

man of mystery exited. Matt and Kerise watched as he made his way across the tarmac, not to the terminal, but toward a parking lot.

"Oh, good, she's there," breathed Kerise. "They didn't get her."

Matt squinted. "The short blonde standing by the brown Chevy?" he said. "She hardly looks old enough to drive."

"She's my age," said Kerise.

"Which is what?"

She admitted to twenty-four. "Anastasia Louise Somerville," she told him. "Analou. Five-foot-two, eyes of blue, just like the old song. She might weigh ninety pounds. One of our Watchers saw her lift a Silverado off a man who'd been trapped when the jack gave way."

"She's strong."

Kerise laughed. "She lifted it with her mind. I got the call, but went for you first because you were closer, and because... never mind." Her face sobered. "There was one more, but they got him."

"Who?"

"Carlos Renaldo Vega."

Matt's eyes widened. "I *served* with him."

"I know."

"They *killed* him? *Who* killed him? Who or what is this Eche—"

"*Merde!*" swore Kerise. She raised her voice and directed it toward the cockpit. "Jacques, we're made. Be ready to take off the instant they're aboard."

Teague was already hustling the young woman ahead of him. Behind them came two men in dark suits, with pistols drawn. One of the pistols bucked, and Matt realized the men were firing. Teague shoved Analou on ahead, then spun around and opened fire. One man fell, his weapon discharging, and Matt heard a distinct *chink* as the bullet struck the Cessna. Teague fired again, and gave a hand signal to Kerise. Matt dashed to the hatch and located Analou, running but still twenty meters away. He closed his eyes, and drew a breath...

...and Anastasia Louise Somerville lay sprawled in the aisle of the Cessna.

"Jacques!" yelled Kerise. "Go! Now!"

"Teague," cried Matt.

"He'll find us," she assured him, as the airplane began to taxi into takeoff.

"The tower has ordered us to halt," Jacques called back. "I shall do no such thing, of course."

"Just get us out of here."

Matt tried to locate Teague, but the angle of vision had changed. His better judgment told him to sit down and fasten his seat belt, and after another moment of anxiety, he surrendered to it and did so.

Kerise dragged the semi-conscious Analou onto a seat, hooked the belt around her, and dropped onto the adjacent seat. She was still looking out the window as the Cessna lifted off.

⁓⁓

Glum, Matt sat staring out the window at the landscape far below. Over and over he told himself he was crazy to be going along with all this, whatever "all this" was. Abducted, shot at, compelled by dangerous circumstances to utilize his abilities more consciously—he should at least have been allowed to practice first!—and not just to rescue himself, but others around him. Strangers, really. Kerise remained a mysterious quantity. The new arrival, Analou, was totally unknown to him. And people were chasing him, trying to kill him; he supposed that was because of his abilities—but how did they know about them? How did Kerise know? But Kerise had not clarified that. Had explained, really, nothing.

And yet... and yet...

Matt had to admit to himself that this was as exciting a time as he'd had in, well, ages. Not since he and Jesse had...

The seat next to his *plumph*ed. A cool hand touched his arm. Not that he wanted to be touched in that moment, but the hand seemed to transfer a deep affection from her into him. The touch was more reassuring than her words.

She said nothing at first, but after a few moments, when he had yet to look at her, she said, "That was quite a range of emotions that crossed your face."

He nibbled at his lower lip. "I don't know what's going on," he said, feeling as if he had already said this, and not just once. "I don't know what I'm doing, or why I'm doing it."

Her voice came to him as fragile as an old wine. "I think what endeared you to me was not your telekinetic potential, but your human side," she told him, unbidden. "You support three children through *Kinderheim*."

He started to reply, but she placed her fingertips gently over his mouth.

"You're on a minimal budget, *n'est-ce pas*?" she went on, her words lightly accented now, as if her French slip were starting to show. "Too much ramen, and frankly not enough vegetables, although you grow some in a garden out back. But the payments to the children go out first; you live on what remains. The postal clerk noted the address one time when you passed her the envelope. You told her you just wanted to do some good."

Matt had enough. He whirled on her. "How long have you been following me?" he demanded.

Kerise did not pull back. "About a year," she said easily. "That particular conversation was overheard by someone else. I have other duties, *entendu*?" She threw a glance at Somerville, now seated three rows up and still dazed. "Saving her was one. Saving Carlos was another, but Echelon got to him first. I'm sorry, Matt. And I'm sorry for throwing at you a load of disjointed information. I cannot even begin to count the number of questions you might have—as I surely would have, were our situations reversed. But I promised to tell you, and I will keep that promise now."

Matt folded his arms across his chest and leaned back in his seat. His expression challenged her to impress him.

010

Bladensburg, Maryland

Geneva Hartland had already begun pre-packing her office in anticipation of a new administrative assignment. This consisted of inscribing a list on her Palmetto—encrypted, of course—detailing the items she needed to take and those that would require shredding and incineration. Idly she wondered, as she sat at her desk, whether she would be asked again to terminate any of her associates in the Echelon. Doctor Elgin Goode, perhaps, who more than anyone save herself, knew of the paranormal project and all its ramifications. He'd never been one to talk out of turn, but he was loyal to her—or was he loyal to the mission? And if the mission were scrubbed—

Her Palmetto sounded. She frowned at the unknown caller ID. Someone who had her number but was not willing to be identified. She hesitated just a fraction, then set for Record, and answered it.

There were no greetings, no chit-chat, just a simple statement, in a male voice without disguise: "The bodies of Agents Henshaw and Okendo are at the Roswell International Air Center. You may wish to sanitize. How many more agents you lose is up to you."

The caller rang off before Hartland could respond. She sat slack-jawed for half a minute or so before pressing the little button on her desk that summoned Oliver West, the Echelon Chief of Security and her long-time associate.

***

Roswell, New Mexico

"What time is it?" Willis asked again.

Landon glowered at him. "Ten minutes since the last time you asked."

Willis removed his bolo tie and draped it over his knee. "It's hot," he muttered. He undid the top button of his shirt and ran a finger around the inside of the collar. "Where the hell is she?"

"Relax," said Landon. He made foot-fists to improve circulation. "Relax. She'll be back. Nobody leaves the garage door open all day. We wait till she gets inside, we knock on the door, when she opens it we make the touch, we bow a little and wave goodbye as if she had just said no thank you to a couple of missionaries, and we report in."

"I know, I know, I know, I know, I know."

"Just keep in mind why we're here, Dave," Landon went on, unperturbed. "Besides, it could be worse."

"*How?*"

"Could be mosquitoes."

Willis rubbed his arms. "No, thanks." He squinted at the open garage, and added, "Maybe it's a ruse. Maybe she's really home."

"So where's the car?"

"I don't know," said Willis, exasperated. "Maybe she loaned it out. Boyfriend—"

"Hasn't any."

"Mom."

"Deceased."

A touch of anger darkened Willis' face. "It's being repaired. It was stolen! Christ, man, there could be a hundred reasons—"

"All available units," the dispatcher interrupted, amid static, "proceed to the airport. Shots fired. Patrol Supervisor report to airport security."

Landon started the car. "Hundred and one," he said. Tires squealed as they sped away.

<hr>

Mexico-Texas border

"I work in a certain project, which I will describe more fully later," began Kerise. "This project, called Indigo, has need of technology that is well beyond our current state-of-the-art. So far beyond, that I personally fear it will not be developed in my lifetime. My... director is optimistic; I do not share that optimism.

"Therefore, I have come up with a different solution to

our technology problem. I have of course informed my, ah, director of this solution—which he regards as a pipe dream, by the way—and he authorized me to pursue it. Which is to say, to pursue you, and Analou, and Carlos. By now it should be obvious that we have access to data and to assets that enable us to conduct this pursuit, among other activities. We have in fact some fifty-four billion euros at our disposal.

"But money, data, and assets cannot provide us with the technology we require in order to complete Indigo."

"That's where I come in," said Matt.

"*Précisement,*" smiled Kerise. "That is where you come in."

Analou shook her head. "But how?" she asked. "I am a geologist. I study strata and sediments. You can find millions of people like me."

"In fact, only three that we know of," replied Kerise. "Two, now."

"No," said Matt.

The tip of Analou's index finger rubbed her snub nose. Her eyes narrowed. "I still don't understand."

Kerise was looking at Matt. "No? Just like that?"

"Some people I don't know are after me," he pointed out. "Now that I know about them, I can deal with them. Whatever you're doing, it's probably illegal—"

"*C'est vrai.* It most certainly is."

"And while that doesn't necessarily put me off, the fact is that I have something I need to do, and it doesn't involve you."

"Isn't that the Rio Grande?" asked Analou, looking out the window.

"Welcome to Mexico," said Kerise. "We'll be putting down at a small airport in the Chihuahua mountains in about half an hour."

"You smuggle drugs," Analou said bitterly, her face reflecting her disappointment.

"Jacques has done," admitted Kerise. "I don't. I won't. We'll wait there for Teague while we refuel, and then press on to Vera Cruz."

Matt was shaking his head.

Kerise touched his arm. "We need you with us," she

said quietly. "I cannot tell you why in sound-bytes; that is why I am slow with details for you. Indigo is bigger than you can imagine. What I can do is show you—"

"No," Matt said again, and vanished.

Analou cried out. Kerise swore venomously in French.

Jacques emerged from the cockpit, a lit cigarette dangling from his mouth. "What has happened?" he said, his accent thick and guttural. "The weight in the plane has shifted."

"We lost Porter," said Kerise.

Under the brim of his desert camouflage bush hat, Jacques' hard gray eyes were suddenly alert. "Do you wish me to go back?" he wanted to know.

Kerise shook her head. "I don't know where he might have gone. Proceed on to the airfield. You and Analou will wait there until I make contact with you."

"I cannot wait," objected Jacques. "I have a shipment to pick up," he glanced meaningfully at Analou, "further south."

"It will be postponed," Kerise told him.

"Only Charteuse can order such a thing."

Kerise flashed a crisp smile. "*Je suis elle-même.*"

011

Munich, Germany

As soon as Langford answered the call on the Palmetto, Henri Montclair snapped, "Where and when did you take that selfie?"

Langford's heart jumped. Now what? "At the Munich *Tiergarten* a couple hours ago. Why? Who is she? What's going on?"

"*Merde!*" swore Montclair. His sharp, dark brown eyes flared with irritation. "Then she is *longtemps* gone." He paused, gathering himself, dragging a thick hand over his salt-and-pepper hair. "What did she say to you?" he demanded. "Tell me what she said. Tell me everything."

Langford straightened the Palmetto on the writing table while he took a moment to think. Montclair's agitation clearly showed in his thick accent; normally he spoke English with only a slight nasal trace. Whoever the young woman in the selfie was, she had Langford's Interpol contact on high alert.

"Henri, you know I have to protect my sources," he said.

"Not in Europe. Not there in Germany. Don't make me dispatch agents, Evan."

Langford sighed. "She gave me a flash drive—"

"Where is it?"

"Who is she?" the journalist shot back.

Montclair's expression said he was drumming his fingers on a table top. The knife scar that ran from his left temple to his left nostril paled with his frustration. Finally he said, "That face matched the one in the only known photograph of a young woman who goes by the code name of Chartreuse. She is a killer and a smuggler, and highly skilled in both fields. You are fortunate to have survived the encounter. I can think of at least seven people who did not."

"Jesus! Who *is* she? And what would she want with *me*?"

Montclair shook his head. "Your turn. And incidentally, GPS has a track on your Palmetto. I know where you are."

"That's not necessary, Henri. You know I'll cooperate, as far as I can." He made a face, and continued. "My turn. All right, she told me not to release whatever is on that flash drive until August 27th this year."

"Did she say why?"

"No. Does the date mean something to you?"

Montclair frowned. "Nothing springs to mind. That's a Friday, it says here."

"I know. I checked. And she added a dire warning against premature disclosure. Tell me who she is, Henri. Off the record. You know me; you have my word on that."

"*Eh bien.* Her real name is Kerise Jeanne Renaud. Ah, I see by your face you know who she is."

"Simon-Louis Renaud's missing daughter."

"In fact, the daughter is merely elusive. It is the father who is missing. The *Sûreté* would like to speak with him about a matter of taxes."

"I can't help you there," said Langford. "She said nothing about him."

"I want to see that flash drive."

"I'm in room 524," Langford told him; unnecessarily, he thought. "Bring a cryptotech."

"See you at ten tomorrow."

Columbus, Ohio

The brownfield corner in Columbus, Ohio, represented the state's economy perfectly. Formerly a gasoline station, the pumps had been removed and the remaining fuel recovered from the underground tanks. The convenience store associated with the station now lay bare, its windows shattered by vandals, its walls tagged by idlers who had run out of train cars on which to stake their artistic claims. A scrawny black and white cat slunk around a corner, hoping it would not be noticed. Here and there a candy wrapper fluttered in the light breeze that swept across the intersection. Stop lights, no longer needed to control the minimal traffic, now blinked red, and more often than not were ignored—glitters of headlight and window glass on the pavement attested to that.

The wind picked up. Under the brown windbreaker, Matt hunched his shoulders and drew the collar up, before stuffing his hands into his pockets. Grit peppered him as he scuffed around the now-vacant lot, searching for the caps to the holes for measuring fuel levels in the two tanks. These were fitted flush to the pavement, and could be opened with the aid of a tire iron or a sturdy screwdriver. Matt found it ironic that the imprint on the caps was that of a foundry in Columbus—a foundry that had gone out of business a decade ago, unable to compete with China.

He dropped to one knee and pried loose a cap. Leaning closer, he sniffed the air. Weak gasoline fumes stung his nostrils and eyes. His lips tight, he rose, nodding to himself. His initial scouting concluded, he entered the convenience store. Moments later, he whispered, "Soon, Jesse. Soon," and disappeared—

...to emerge scant seconds later by a dumpster in an alley behind a deserted store at a strip mall in a Columbus suburb. Across the street stood a Big Box home improvement depot. There he bought an eight-foot length of pine flashing and a can of lighter fluid. These he paid for by debit card, and was relieved to find that his account had not as yet been frozen.

Upon his return to the abandoned gas station, Matt dropped the flashing into the fuel level hole, noting that it reached the bottom about seven feet down. He gave the wood several squirts of lighter fluid, so that it trickled down into the fuel tank. He then laid a trail of lighter fluid from the hole to the convenience store, where he ducked inside.

Here goes, he thought, and used a Bic lighter to inflame the trail.

The *whoomp* that followed several seconds later was louder than he had anticipated, but the explosion did not disturb the pavement. The flashing shot upwards, and soon clattered back onto the concrete.

Step one, Matt told himself, and again vanished, to reappear this time near a sporting goods store in La Jolla,

Indigo

California.

<hr>

Chihuahua, Mexico

"He got away," said Kerise, on the scrambled Palmetto. "There's something else going on with him. He has an agenda."

The voice in reply spoke the Queen's English, but with a French accent. "What have you told him so far?"

Her face showed annoyance as she looked at the make-shift clandestine air strip in the badlands of Chihuahua. "What you authorized me to say: bare bones." She sighed. "Matt has his own problems, Papa. As I advised you he would. He has no room to care for ours, especially when I have to be so vague about them."

"So you told me. *Eh bien.* If you can locate him again, tell him whatever you think he should know."

"*When* I find him," said Kerise. "I will."

"How, may I ask?"

"The government hasn't frozen his debit and credit cards as yet," she said. "I'm monitoring, so even if they do, I can unblock them. Eventually he will use one of them, and it will give me a place to start." She paused briefly. "Has any progress been made on your primary propulsion system?"

"No. And time is growing short." Weariness showed in his voice and in his face in the screen. "It may not be possible, Kerise. We may have to go with something generational."

She shook her head. "Matt can do it," she assured him. "I just have to persuade him."

She rang off, and watched a dust devil maneuver across the runway. It dashed itself against the Cessna, and recovered on the other side, whirling onward. The symbolism felt familiar, but elusive. She pondered it a moment, and shrugged. It occurred to her then that one of the best ways to grasp something mentally was to clear the mind, ignore it, and wait for it to manifest itself. Perhaps that was true of Matt Porter as well. If she had more time available, she might have waited him out. If.

Her Palmetto pinged. She had set it to alert her whenever Matt used his plastic. She tapped for the activity, and frowned. Columbus, Ohio, and San Diego, California.

Qu'est-ce que fais-tu? she thought. What is it that you are you doing?

La Jolla Cove, California

There was something tranquilizing, even hypnotic, thought Matt, about steady ocean waves. They washed up, they died, they retreated. Over and over again, for hundreds of millions of years. Rocks pounded to sand. Shells smashed to calcium carbonate. Shorelines eroded.

Lulled by the roar of the waves and the warmth of the night, Matt closed his eyes. He longed to secure himself inside the womb of sleep, but it evaded the grasp of his calm, taunting him. Abandoning the attempt, he gazed out to left of center, at the islet of rocks off the promontory. There, over seventy years ago, a sixteen-foot great white shark had devoured an unwary swimmer. Years later, the shark was caught and killed; an examination of the contents of the digestive tract turned up the swimmer's wristwatch.

Justice.

He had to be as cold as a great white, as dispassionate as a medical examiner. Not until he had captured and incarcerated Jesse's killer could he afford to vent his wrath, his rage. For tonight, he allowed himself to soak up the peace of the ocean.

He heard the chuff of sand before he felt the approaching footsteps. A steady but cautious approach, as if the person were uncertain of how she would be received. Yes, she, he decided; it could only be a girl in such a clichéd circumstance.

Bare feet, and legs clad in black denims like his own, came into view as she carefully sat down beside him. Not too far away; just outside arm's reach. Matt turned his head a little. Royal blue string bikini top, the contents not too abundant. Tanned skin. Heart-shaped face framed by long black hair and dominated by large dark eyes. Pert nose, petite mouth; a flicker of smile. An anime princess incarnate.

Matt returned his attention to the whitecaps marching in echelon to die on the shore, like phalanxes of soldiers tromping into machine-gun fire. The imagery stemmed from Jesse, from the manner of his murder. Matt shook his head to clear it; his chest rose and fell in a deep, prolonged sigh.

She had brought a blanket with her. She rose to her knees and spread it out on the sand, and moved to the far side of it, implicitly inviting him to take the near side, if he so desired. Legs tucked under her, she sat back and waited for him.

He counted five other people on the cove beach. Surely she couldn't intend that he and she...

Maybe she saw that he needed something. What was that line from Longfellow? *Ships that pass in the night, and speak each other in passing,* was it? *Only a look and a voice, then darkness again and a silence?* Maybe she saw that he needed that look and a voice. He scooted onto the blanket, once again just outside arm's reach of her, and returned his gaze to the ocean.

Silence reigned between them. Perhaps she did not know what to say to him, while he was content merely to know that she was there. It gave him peace in the same way the waves soothed him. That was enough.

Time counted. Presently—an hour later? Two hours?— she said, very softly, "Were you going to stay out here all night? Alone?"

He could but nod.

"Shall I leave you the blanket?" she asked. "I can come get it in the morning."

He did not answer.

"I have a Volkswagen camper parked at the top of the hill," she told him. "It has a bed. It's comfortable." Quickly she added, "But we don't have to do anything."

But they did.

In the morning Matt awoke, alone on the blanket, on the beach, with no memory of how he had come to be there. He glanced up and back: the VW was gone. *Only a look and a voice, then darkness again and a silence.* But it was the echo of his own voice that he heard. A name he had called out while in the throes.

Kerise.

012

Bladensburg, Maryland

Despite the internal security of the Echelon building, Geneva Hartland had her office swept for listening and recording devices each morning after her arrival. Today was no different, and the results were the same, as always: secure. But the rogue agent code-named Teague knew her personal contact number, and who knew what else he had access to. After discussing the matter yesterday with Oliver West, her Chief of Security, she had debated whether to move her office—several other rooms in the old building were empty—and concluded that it was more prudent to remain where she was and assume surveillance, even if so far it had gone undetected. In this way—assuming surveillance—Echelon could if desired control the information that might be overheard. The deviousness, though a common practice in counter-espionage, appealed to Hartland.

After knocking, and receiving permission to enter, Oliver West stepped into the office, looking as furtive as ever. He reminded Hartland of Peter Lorre, who gave the impression of always looking over his shoulder, even when facing straight ahead. His hunched shoulders under the light brown suit jacket said that he expected a blow from behind at any moment. Hartland bade him seat himself, offered him a drink that she knew he would refuse, and sat down behind her desk, folding her hands on top of the blotter. Her expression said, "Well?"

"Confirmed misses on Somerville and Porter," he announced. "The whereabouts of Somerville is not known at this time."

Hartland perked up at the omission. "And Porter?"

"His debit card showed up yesterday evening in Columbus, Ohio, and San Diego." West paused to throw a quick glance over his shoulder. "The purchases were made an hour and twenty-seven minutes apart. That's hyper-sonic."

Hartland's lips tightened, bloodless. "Or," she said.

West nodded. "Or," he agreed, adding, "I can freeze his assets."

Hartland considered this, and shook her head. "We need real-time notification whenever he uses his plastic," she said. "With that, we can track him. Maybe we'll get lucky." She hesitated. "It's almost as if he doesn't care whether he can be traced."

"I noticed that."

"Maybe he'll get careless. What did he buy?"

"Some flashing and lighter fluid in Columbus," West answered. "Some SCUBA gear in San Diego."

Hartland sat back, puzzled. "What on Earth?"

"My thought, exactly," said West. He started to say more, and stopped, uncertain.

"What little thought crossed your mind just then, Oliver?"

His left hand rubbed the arm of the stuffed chair. "Well... SCUBA gear is relatively easy to buy on the coasts," he said slowly. "Florida, California. But lighter fluid is available anywhere. There's no need to carry it around with you."

Hartland frowned heavily. "It's unlikely he's lugging SCUBA gear around."

"Not what I was getting at," West said, diffident now. "He used the lighter fluid, or he has a use for it, in Columbus. Whatever he's going to do, it'll be in Columbus."

"And it involves SCUBA gear."

"Which could get him noticed."

"Get us some boots on the ground, Oliver," she ordered. "Coordinate with HomeSec and the FBI. Report anything unusual, no matter how small."

"That could be a lot of unrelated reports," West pointed out.

"That's why we have analysts, Oliver."

Munich, Germany

Langford had already received room service in the form of coffee and bread rolls with butter by the time Montclair and the tech arrived. The latter was a tall and skinny woman introduced only as Sylvie. Her plain face, framed by a cap of short black hair, was devoid of cosmetics. She hid her eyes behind tinted glasses and what there was of her figure under a white blouse and brown vest and a sepia pencil skirt. She wore tan loafers. Langford estimated her age at two years either way of thirty. As Montclair was known to select his section's female personnel on the basis of appearance as well as expertise, Langford concluded that Sylvie was one highly skilled tech.

She laid her Palmetto on the table. "Have you the flash drive?" she asked, in a heavy French accent.

Langford handed it to her. His laptop was already powered up. She sat down before it, and slipped the drive into the port. Within seconds she removed her glasses and clanked them down on the table, staring hard at the monitor. Finally she sat back, and muttered something in rapid French that swept right on by Langford.

He looked to Montclair, who translated, "This thing is so highly encrypted it makes the hackers in China and North Korea look like retired arithmetic teachers."

"Or words to that effect, I suppose," added Langford. Montclair grinned and nodded, and he went on, "Can she decrypt it?"

"I do speak the English," snapped Sylvie, inserting a drive of her own. "It is that I am told this came from a member of the Renaud family."

"*C'est vrai,*" Langford confirmed. "Can you decrypt it?"

"I am making the copy of it now, to take to the lab." Suddenly she leaned closer. "Hmm."

"*Qu'est-ce que passe?*" asked Montclair.

"The drive has transmitted the signal."

"Unplug it," urged Langford.

Sylvie shook her head. "It is too late." Several seconds later, she removed both drives, and returned the original to Langford. "*C'est possible,*" she told him, but looked doubtful.

Langford scarcely heard her. She had glistening azure eyes—or she was wearing tinted lenses. The effect on him was the same, either way. Mentally his knees buckled.

"It is that the signal was sent to the Renaud family," she went on, resetting her glasses as she stood up. "They now know the attempt has been made to read this."

"I would still like to know the significance of that date," said Montclair. "I was hoping that drive would tell us. She said nothing at all about it?"

Langford picked up a bread roll, looked it over, and set it back down. "I've told you everything," he said peevishly. "The entire encounter lasted maybe half a minute." He looked to Sylvie. "If it's encrypted, how am I supposed to read it?"

She shrugged, and began to butter the roll he had examined. "It is that the encryption has the timer set into it," she said. "This is simple enough to do, for the Renauds."

"Sylvie is still trying to decrypt the Renaud Corporation financial data," explained Montclair.

She made a face. "Without the success." About to add a remark, she paused. Her upper incisors caught on her lower lip. Montclair made an inviting gesture, and she went on, "The recipient of the signal will be able to trace the location of the source. If it is that I can reverse the trace, it is possible I can locate the source of it."

Montclair considered this. "You would have to be here to do that," he pointed out.

"*Oui, c'est vrai.*"

"Now, wait just a minute," Langford protested.

Montclair cut him off. "My job is to find Simon Renaud," he said. "This may be the best opportunity I've had so far." To Sylvie he added, "Before I return to Brussels, I'll arrange the adjacent room for you. The porter will bring up your travel bag. If something develops, notify me immediately."

After Montclair closed the door behind him, Langford turned to Sylvie, who had devoured half the bread roll. "Can you really do all this stuff you say you can?" he asked.

She swallowed, and gave him a wan smile. "I was not

hired for the looks."

"I didn't mean—" he began, and broke off, not quite certain what it was that he did not mean. "Do you have to stay here? I mean, in here?"

Her thin shoulders shrugged. "It is that the laptop must be watched."

"Yes," sighed Langford. "Yes, of course. Why not take it into your room?"

"Is it that I am so ill-favored?"

The abrupt question startled him into a shocked silence.

"You may calm yourself," she said evenly. "I do not have the designs on you."

"So I'm ill-favored, then?"

Her jaw dropped. Then she burst out laughing.

Langford invited her to reseat herself at the desk. "Do whatever you have to do," he said. "Is there any danger of losing my own files?"

She pursed her thin lips, uncertain. "*C'est possible*," she allowed. "Have you the backup?"

"In a Cloud."

"Tchah!" She muttered something that Langford did not catch, and struck several keys, studying the results. From a vest pocket she withdrew another flash drive, checked the capacity, and slipped it into the computer. Another tocking of keys brought up a small transfer window, across which a narrow green line slowly moved. "Anyone can gain the access to the Cloud," she said, none too gently. Her tone added that he should have known that.

"So I should use a physical backup as well."

"*Précisement.* It is not the perfect system, but it is much more secure than the Cloud." The download completed, she handed him the drive. "The vulnerability increases with the *technologique*—the, ah, complexity. *Regardez*—consider the automobile. It is that you use it to go to places, *n'est-ce pas*? But you have the toys: the windows that open and close on command, the *odometre* to tell you how far you may travel on the gasoline you have remaining, the adjustable *miroir*. You do not need them to go to the store, or to Bordeaux. They are toys. The more toys in any *technologie*, the more can go wrong."

Langford chuckled. "I should find you a soap box."

Heavy black eyebrows lifted. "Soap box? What is the soap box?"

"For your speech."

Her eyes said she still did not comprehend.

"Never mind," he said. "It is just a saying. Would you care for something else from room service?"

She shook her head. "Order what you wish."

He was about to do so when they heard a knock on the door—four quick raps of the knuckles.

Instantly Sylvie was on her feet, an automatic pistol in her right hand. Langford had not seen her draw it, but the hem of her skirt fell back into place when she stood up. She stepped to one side of the door, and made a little gesture for him to open it.

013

French Lick, Indiana

The best that could be said of the motel, thought Matt, was that as far as he could tell it was devoid of roaches and bedbugs. The concave mattress on the twin bed looked lumpy. Someone had removed the Gideon Bible from the nightstand. The lamp on the stand was too far away from the outlet to plug in—he moved it to the simple veneer dresser, and found that the bulb had died. At least the overhead and bathroom lights worked.

He sat down at the desk; the chair, at least, was sturdier than it looked. On top of the desk was a calendar card, and a writing pad with the motel's logo as letterhead, and a ball point pen that he soon discovered was out of ink. Daylight still filtered through the thin blue curtains, the sun an hour from setting.

His eyes settled on the items on the floor in the open closet—SCUBA gear, some hand tools, a set of large screw eyes, a coil of yellow nylon rope, a plastic canteen. Several other items he would eventually require had to be obtained surreptitiously, under the cover of darkness. In the meantime, his plans had firmed. He had no need to review them again. He was focused on the items because he was trying not to think about Kerise Renaud.

Which meant that he was unable to erase her from his mind.

She possessed a skill set that, when he considered it, left him stunned. She seemed to be in control of whatever resources she required, be they airplanes or vehicles or personnel. She had a plan, and knew how to execute it. He, however, was the pebble in her shoe. She had known beforehand of his telekinetic potential. She had not realized just how advanced he had grown. And she was so engrossed in her own strategies that she had not considered that he might have his own purposes, his own objectives.

Still, what could she possibly want with him? It

concerned his potential, that much was certain. But she was also attracted to him—to a man she had only read about in classified files and dossiers. Attracted to the extent of bedding him.

Life around her was frenetic. When he thought back on it, he realized that he had enjoyed the relief from his everyday dudgeon. What was that quote from Churchill, after the Boer War? Nothing was more exhilarating than to be shot at without effect? Something like that. But first: Jessie. Then, if he survived, he might devote some attention to Kerise's project, whatever it was.

⁕

Chihuahua, Mexico

In the high desert of Chihuahua State, Kerise fumed. All but one point of her plan had succeeded. She'd gotten Matt Porter away from Echelon in time. They'd acquired Somerville along the way, rescuing her in the nick of time. They'd gotten out of the country, thanks in no small measure to Teague. But she hadn't counted on Porter's telekinetic development. That was supposed to have taken place after she'd gotten him to Brazil. Something had caused it to develop prematurely. And she had no idea what it might have been, and no way to restrain him.

Now all she could do was await events. Having spent one night aboard the Cessna, she did not relish spending another. The late afternoon air at this altitude had already begun to chill her. She rubbed her bare arms, and scuffed at the red sandstone beneath her feet.

"He's all over the place," said Teague, standing beside her as the sun poised above the mountains in preparation for its daily dip. "San Diego, Columbus twice, French Lick. And you can be sure that—"

"French Lick?"

"It's in southern Indiana," Teague told her. "Known for mineral springs and Larry Bird. Why?"

A thought had flitted past her mind, evading capture. "What was the sequence?" she asked.

"Columbus, San Diego, Columbus, French Lick. *M'selle* Renaud, I'm not sure I follow your thinking."

59

She shook her head at herself. "It's probably nothing."

"At this point, any clue might be helpful," he prodded.

"Well..." Her face warmed. "He knows I'm French."

Teague did not voice a vulgar comment, for which she was grateful. "A signal, do you suppose?"

Her only response was to watch the sun sink for a few seconds. "Twice in Columbus, you said?" she went on. "Whatever he means to do, it's there. *C'est là-bas.* Go tell Jacques to prepare a flight for a small airport near French Lick, and ask Analou to come out here."

Moments later, the young woman from Roswell arrived. She was still wearing the smudged white jersey and the blue jean cutoffs that she had slept in. Kerise sympathized with her. Everyone in the group needed a bath and a change of clothes, and a good night's sleep, and until she could come up with a plan of action, none of them were likely to get those.

"How's your ESP?" she asked Analou.

Shivering a little after she threw a glance at the departing Teague, the geologist tilted her head back to meet Kerise's eyes, and gave a noncommittal response. "It needs work."

"What about range? Can you read someone from a thousand miles away?"

She smiled tolerantly. "It doesn't quite work like that," she answered. "Try to imagine six billion voices, and being able to single out one. It's like being a penguin in Antarctica, listening for her baby's voice. The problem is that the penguins can do it. We ourselves can't even begin to imagine how that is possible. With considerable practice, yes, at some point I suppose I'd be able to do it. That's probably why they want to kill me."

Kerise frowned. "I thought they simply feared your abilities," she said. "I didn't realize they had a specific reason."

"Suppose I could read the mind of the President, or the Secretary of Defense, or of some foreign leader," Analou explained. "Imagine what an asset I'd be to almost any country. Or suppose I read a football coach, and pass on the plays he calls to the opposing coach. Las Vegas and Reno would send every hit man they had against me. No, I already had a plan to disappear. I knew eventually they'd come for me. When you called the other day, I read your mind. I knew you were on the level." She paused as the lower edge of the sun began to pass behind the mountains. The sky above it, already red and salmon, began to take on some lavender streaks. "Beautiful," she breathed.

Kerise hesitated. "How much of me did you see?" she asked, her breath bated.

"Not everything," Analou admitted. "I'm well aware that in time the only way I'll be allowed to remain alive is if I keep my mouth shut. And 'read' is not really the best word. I detect emotions and images. At some point I may be able to transmit them as well."

Kerise considered this. "*Alors*, you were able to read me because you were locked into me on the phone," she mused. "If I can get you close enough, do you think you could lock in on someone else?"

"On Matt, you mean?" Her lips curled in a secret smile. "I think so. If you can get me close enough."

Kerise turned her and nudged her toward the Cessna. "Go fasten your seat belt," she said, grinning. "Make sure your seat is in the upright position."

Bladensburg, Maryland

There's no such thing as a weekend, thought Geneva Hartland, as she returned with a mug of cafeteria coffee to her usual place, behind her desk. Half an hour earlier she had received a report from Oliver West regarding the movements of Matthew Porter. If there was a method to his meandering, she was unable to discern it. San Diego, Columbus, and French Lick. She was unable to think of anything that might link the cities.

The digital clock on her monitor rolled over to 1900 hours. Two hours of daylight left. She thought of the cot in the closet off to the right; she didn't mind sleeping on it— she'd done so on too many occasions to count—but she hated to set up the framework.

As if on cue, West entered her office, without

invitation, earning a deep frown from her that faded as soon as she saw the expression on his face. Had the analysts made some sense out of all those unsorted reports? A gesture from her bade him sit down.

"Tell me good news, Oliver," she said.

He shook his head sadly. "It's not that, exactly," he hedged. "We've been looking at Porter's movements with the wrong eyes."

"Don't go all squishy on me, Oliver," she warned.

"No, Doctor," he said, reverting to the honorific to acknowledge her position. "We've been tracking him in order to be able to anticipate his movements, so that we can eliminate the threat he poses. But we have not assessed that threat, and it is the consensus of Analysis that he is on the verge of using his powers to serve his personal agenda."

"And what would that be, Oliver?"

He looked flustered. "Well, I-I don't know for certain."

"Then *guess*," she snapped. In a calmer voice, she added, "Just give me something I can work with."

West laid a document on her desk. The cover had the luminescent copper border and the security warning PARANORMAL SECRET EYES ONLY. Carefully, as if it might explode, he pushed it closer to her. "Porter's PsychEval," he announced.

"I've read it."

"Not this document. I only found out about it an hour ago. Doering in Analysis had it."

"Summarize," she instructed, as she slipped the warning cover from the top page.

West responded as if he had already rehearsed what he was about to say.

"Matthew Porter and his younger brother Jesse enlisted in the United States Army right after the ricin attack at the Super Bowl four years ago," he began. "Both were sent to the reopened Defense Language School in Monterey, California, to learn Arabic, the Syrian dialect. Upon completion, both were assigned to combat units in Afghanistan. And don't ask. You may recall that during the Viet Nam war, intel analysts were taught Vietnamese and then sent to Germany, while those who spoke German wound up in Saigon."

"I recall no such thing," Hartland said stiffly. "Continue, please."

"In Afghanistan, both men became disaffected with the war. After eight months in-country, the elder Porter was wounded in action and was MEDEVACed to Germany, where his EEG showed indicators that alerted Echelon. From there he was ordered to Fort Holabird for, ah, testing, and subsequently released on a disability. The direct deposit also enabled us to keep track of his address. The younger brother remained at a base near Kabul, where he was killed during an infiltration."

"So far I've heard nothing—"

"The psychological evaluation the elder Porter underwent at Holabird showed an intense need to protect his younger brother. After Jesse was killed, Matthew formed a fixed delusion that he had let Jesse down. The evaluation strongly suggested that he would attempt to avenge his brother's death. Against whom, is the question."

Finished, West sat back, arms folded across his chest as if to ward off a rebuke from Hartland for having interrupted her. Yet her face showed no sign of hostility; rather, an air of thoughtfulness gave her a million-mile look as she stared above West's head.

"Matthew Porter was born in Columbus, Ohio," Hartland said at last. "What about the younger brother?"

"Also born in Columbus."

For long seconds, neither spoke. She gazed placidly at West and broke the heavy silence. "Go ahead with your conclusion," she urged. "You've done the work."

West ticked the points off on his fingers. "One, he'll take his revenge in Columbus. Two, it will be massive."

"Very well, let's assume that." Hartland paused briefly. "We're not staffed to monitor an entire city. Let's bring the Bureau in on this; they have the personnel. I'll make the call. In the meantime, divert the EMUs to Columbus."

"What do we do about Somerville?"

"Am I correct in thinking that she has no motivation to do harm?"

West's lips puffed out. "As far as we know," he conceded. "Yes."

"Continue to monitor her movements, insofar as that is possible. Plastic, passport, the works. When we've finished the Porter, we'll resume the Somerville." She gestured toward the file. "Leave that here. I'll secure it before I leave."

West rose. "Doctor," he said, with a slight bow, and departed.

Alone, Hartland grumbled to herself. Of the three individuals, none had known they were targets. Yet two of them had contrived to escape the EMUs. The Commit order had to be carried out. There was no other way for her to expunge the failures from her record.

Why Columbus? she thought. *What horrible deed could he perpetrate in the brownfields of Columbus, Ohio?*

014

French Lick, Indiana

Kerise had to admit that Teague looked unrecognizable in a black hairpiece and make-up eyebrows. Not much could be done to disguise his burly shoulders, but he managed to walk as if he were a few inches shorter than his listed six-two. The Glock in the rig under his left arm might have been noticeable to another professional, but here in French Lick nobody was paying attention. For all they knew, Kerise, Teague, and Analou were tourists, a father and his two daughters, here for the springs or the Bird Museum or even just passing through.

After taking two rooms at a motel, they had gone out for breakfast, and now were wandering around a strip mall in search of the drugstore where Matthew Porter had bought a pair of vodka miniatures and a bag of chocolate chip cookies the evening before. From time to time Kerise reset her earbud, more from habit than from necessity, to be certain in this instance of maintaining communication with Jacques at the airport outside town.

"You're going to make it noticeable," Teague cautioned her, while they pretended to examine the wares in a health and nutrition shop.

"Is someone watching?" asked Kerise. Practiced in the nuances of counter-surveillance, she had not spotted any-one of interest among the fifty or so shoppers. She sighed. "But you're right. Still, there must be others around here with earbuds. They aren't that unusual. In any event, Matt will notice me before he focuses on my ear."

"I don't see anyone watching us," said Teague. "But that doesn't mean they aren't."

The tip of Analou's tongue moistened her chapped lips. "I could use a tube of lip-balm," she said.

She entered the shop, made a quick selection, and paid for it in cash. When she returned, her right canine teeth were working the lining of her mouth.

"I sense something," she said softly to Kerise. "But I'm

not able to bring it into focus."

"Is it Matt?" she asked.

"I-I think so."

"Just relax," said Teague, as they moved along the strip. "Let it come to you. Kerise, the drugstore is three doors down."

"So I see. Analou, is he here?"

"No. But..."

Kerise pulled up. "But?"

Analou's fingers shagged her short blonde hair. "I don't know, I don't know," she complained. "Just a feeling, an omen. Something dark, black. Something nearby, very close." She blinked, and threw a sidelong glance at Teague. Then her eyes bored into Kerise. "I'm a novice right now," she said evenly. "I don't know how to decipher everything I receive, everything I sense. There's something wrong; that's all I know. And I don't think it has anything to do with Ma—with him."

"Take your time," Teague soothed.

Her desert-tanned face twisted as if she had just felt a twinge of pain. "It's not a question of time," she snapped at him. "It's like a premonition. A glimpse of evil. Something very bad has begun."

"Here?" he pressed. "Has it begun here?"

"I don't know," she wailed. "Oh, I don't know."

"Let her alone," said Kerise. She gestured toward a fast-food restaurant. "Let's go over there and relax," she suggested. "We'll have something to eat, then check out the chemist's—I mean, the drugstore."

Moments later found them at a booth inside, where they had a clear view of the drugstore. Each had a beverage at hand, and Kerise was addressing herself to a biscuit with an egg, a slice of cheese, and a sausage patty. Analou looked a little pale now, but seemed to have calmed herself. Teague, vigilant, did not take his eyes from the store.

People wandered in and out. By the time Kerise finished her biscuit, it was past eleven. The urge to push Analou a little harder grew to the point where it was almost overwhelming. Was Matthew Porter here in French Lick, or not? If he was, then where? And of course, if he wasn't, then where? The petite blonde woman seemed relaxed now. Perhaps she was more effective in that state.

Suddenly Analou looked up, with pale, wild eyes. In the same moment, a goateed and unkempt young man who might have been a college student, given the textbooks under one arm, pointed to an object on the floor near the doorway.

"Hey, did someone leave their backpack outside?"

Teague's face blanched as he shot to his feet. "Don't touch it!" he yelled. To Kerise, he said, "Take Analou and get out of here. Get as far away as you can."

Bewildered, Kerise could only frown. "What—"

Analou moaned, and pressed her hands to her head.

Teague gave them no time to reply. He surged outside toward the backpack.

Comprehension smote Kerise. *"Mon Dieu!"* she whispered hoarsely.

⁂

Teague was just aware of Kerise and Analou following in his wake. Some customers milled about, dumbfounded; others scattered. Outside, the reactions were similar. He had no time for them, not now. They had been warned. He spotted the blue backpack leaning against the great front window of the restaurant. It had been ideally positioned to create as much glass shrapnel as possible. Someone bumped him, setting his heightened senses on edge. Kerise; he whirled on her.

"Damn it, I *told* you—"

She made a sweeping gesture at the gathering throng. "Tell *them*," she snapped. "They think this is a game."

While she and Analou tried to shoo the crowd away, and only half-successful, Teague dropped to his knees beside the backpack. It looked innocuous enough. There was every chance it was what it appeared to be. Someone had forgotten it, and would be back for it. That sort of thing happened all the time. Sometimes people even forgot their children.

He performed a swift but thorough examination of the canvas exterior. It was misshapen by its contents; he was unable to determine what they might be. Even as he watched, something inside the backpack began to move, ever so slightly. His heart stammered. A cloud of fear engulfed him, and he blew it aside. Later there would be time for it. Later. With the caution of a demolitions expert, he lifted the loose flap. It revealed nothing; he would have to open the pack further in order to inspect the contents.

Still, the movement. Something round; it might be the detonator. Teague could think of no reason for it to be moving, but IEDs came in all shapes and sizes. His fingers crawled toward the opening at the top of the pack.

An orange head appeared there: a ginger cat. Teague felt weak, destabilized. The cat had clots of pink on its nose and whiskers. It took him a few seconds to figure out what it was: tuna fish, undoubtedly from someone's lunch inside. He could smell it. As if frightened by the people standing around, the cat jerked itself from the backpack and took off running.

Behind him, Kerise hissed in annoyance. In French. One of the words sounded like "shah." French for "cat." He had no doubt an adjective or two accompanied the noun.

False alarm, he started to say, but training remained with him. He gently pried open the pack and saw the bomb.

"Get them out of here," he told Kerise, his voice low.

"Is that—"

"Yes. For once in your lucking fife, obey me."

She spoke a few words. He could not make out, nor did he care, what they were, but people started running. He peered further inside the pack, not as concerned for movement as he might have been. After all, the cat hadn't set the thing off. He saw a roundish pile of nuts, bolts, fragments of metal, shards of glass. A pair of wires led into it. He decided not to dislodge them yet; almost certainly there was a glob of C4 within. The apparatus appeared to be unsophisticated. But the wires were also attached to— his heart stopped—a *receiver*.

He did not look around; he did not have to. Of a certainty someone was watching, was already pulling out a smart phone. He had no choice, not now. Cringing, he picked up the receiver and pulled the wires free.

Just after he did so, the bare ends of the wires

touched, and a spark passed between them. Teague's stomach felt hollow; nauseous, he swallowed hard, and looked around for anyone on the periphery with a phone in his hand. About fifty yards away, a bearded man was slipping something into his jacket as he turned to walk away. Teague longed to give chase, but now he had a far more important task.

He stood up and beckoned urgently to Kerise. "Go back and get the car, and meet me in the parking lot," he ordered.

"What are you—"

"I'll explain later. *Please*, Kerise." She glanced down at the backpack and he added, "It's safe now."

She gathered up Analou. "Should I call the police?" she asked.

"I'd rather you didn't. Although they are probably on their way here. Go, go."

To his immense relief, she did not argue. He moved to a secluded spot around the corner from the restaurant, where he could still see the backpack and watch for the arrival of the police, and thumbed a special button on his smart phone.

The answering voice came from an alcove in the Pentagon, near the impact site of American Airlines Flight 77. It belonged to a U. S. Army Lieutenant Colonel in the Pentagon's G-2. He said, simply, "Rother."

"Record, Al," said Teague, and assumed a device had been activated. "See something, say something. I'm saying. There are IEDs positioned outside the main windows or just inside of most chain fast-food restaurants in the country. They'll be in backpacks, shopping bags, old clunker cars. Anonymous, innocuous containers. They are set to go off sometime during the lunch hour. The one I found would have been set off by smart phone. It's a relatively simple device—ball bearings, nuts and bolts, C4."

"Judas fucking Priest."

"By now you know where I am. The backpack is blue. It's safe; you can collect it."

"Other ears, Teague."

"Like I don't know that. But I'm not your problem, Al.

Don't waste time with me." He rang off before Rother could respond.

The police had not arrived yet; he did not even hear a distant siren. Casually he walked to the strip mall's parking lot and climbed into the passenger side of the rental. "Take it easy, Kerise," he told her. He raised his voice as they sped away. "No, just drive. And mind the spucking feed limit."

"Stop!" cried Analou.

Kerise pulled over to the side of the road and looked back at her.

"He's here," she said.

⸎

Kerise's astonishment lasted only a couple seconds. She did not insult the woman by asking if she was sure. "Can you determine where?" she asked.

Analou shook her head uncertainly. "A motel room, I think."

"That narrows it down considerably," grunted Teague.

"It's more than what we had," Kerise snapped. "Analou, can you 'see' anything?"

"Nooo... wait." She shut her eyes; the lids fluttered as if she were receiving a message from beyond.

"This is so Shirley MacLaine," added Teague.

"Shut up!" hissed Analou.

Kerise gave him a hard look. "That's *enough.*"

"I work for your father," said Teague. "Not for you."

Her spine rigid now, she glared at him. She wished she had darts of fire and ice. "Here, I *am* my father." With fierce softness she went on, "You're being well-paid, Teague."

"Yeah." He sighed. "Sorry. A lot of people could be about to die, just like nine-eleven. And there's no more I can do about it."

Kerise reached out and touched his arm. "I know," she said gently, thinking of his loss on that terrible and fateful day. "I know. And I'm sorry as well. But we do what we can. And right now we have a chance to find Matt."

"*Starbright Motel,*" Analou popped up, her eyes wide open now. "I can't see the room number. He's inside. Ah...

70

curtains are drawn."

"What's he doing?" asked Teague.

"He's... ah..." Her face colored. "He's... enthroned."

Laughter seized Kerise. The rental had GPS, and Teague asked it for directions while she recovered. The motel was "one point three eight" miles away. Following instructions, Kerise turned left, just as a police cruiser rushed past them in the other direction, its siren doppler-ing up and then back down. Her mood dampened. She chanced a look at Teague, but his face was impassive as he stared straight ahead. His jaw muscles tightened and relaxed, and tightened again.

Another cruiser sped past, flashing the emergency blue lights. "Your doing, *n'est-ce pas*?" she asked Teague.

"I called it in," he said. "I had to."

"They'll be looking for you."

"It couldn't be helped, Kerise."

She took a hard right, again by instructions. "You did the right thing. I just hope... well, you know."

"Yeah."

"He's gone," Analou said suddenly. "He left. I can't track him."

"Let's get out of here," said Teague.

Kerise shook her head. "No. We check out his room. He may have left something behind." With a glance in the rear-view mirror at Analou, she said, "Something you might be able to trace."

015

Northern Virginia

Inside the Pentagon, eyes were usually the first things to roll in disbelief, often followed by heads. Those of General Gaylord J. Sutcliffe, Deputy Chief of Staff for Intelligence, were arctic blue; his did not roll, but glared at Rother from behind his great mahogany desk. "You're asking me to notify HomeSec to initiate emergency response teams all over the country to prevent or otherwise deal with a coordinated and timed attack on restaurants and probably other locations that are crowded during the time zone's lunch hour."

Rother's heart paced faster. He had no doubt that Teague's warning was actionable. But how to convince the DCI? And do it in mere minutes? If they had that long. Seated in a wooden, castered armchair, he steeled himself for argument. For now, he could only respond, "Yes, sir."

"On the basis of a rogue former CIA agent who is so far out of disfavor with this government that there are standing orders for him to be shot on sight."

"Yes, sir."

The eyes hardened to glacial ice. "You and Hodges were tight, once."

"That won't stop me from shooting him dead, the moment I see him, sir. It won't even make me hesitate."

"He called you," emphasized the general. "Nobody else, just you. He's your conduit into operations."

Rother's spine stiffened beyond attention. "This could be the next nine-eleven, sir."

"Could be. Colonel... *Lieutenant* Colonel, have you any idea of the costs involved in activating a nationwide emergency response?"

"Sir, I prefer to consider the costs of not acting."

The desk intercom buzzed. Sutcliffe hit a button. "Not right now, Gloria," he said tersely.

Rother gazed out the window behind the DCI. It gave onto a view of one of the vast parking lots. Off to the left, out of sight, the grounds damaged by the impact of American Airlines Flight 77 had yet to be fully repaired. The DCI had often commented that their unrepaired condition should serve as a reminder of the event. Rother hoped the DCI was not inviting another reminder. But Teague... *dammit*, Teague had no motive whatsoever for lying. Not considering what happened to his wife and child in the Towers.

Gloria, the receptionist and invaluable scheduler, remained adamant. "It's General Polk, sir."

Sutcliffe grimaced. "Very well. Put him on." He shifted the intercom to commo and gave his last name.

Mentally Rother crossed his fingers, and prayed. He greatly feared that prayer was all that remained now, to him and to the country.

He was aware of some of Polk's frantic words over the speaker phone. First, an advisory: the Pentagon was being locked down. Eight explosions, two each in Baltimore and Tampa, one each in four other major cities. HomeSec was responding... the President is secure... air-raid sirens are...

Too late, thought Rother. He swallowed the acid that stung the back of his throat.

The call ended abruptly. Sutcliffe seized the silence to raise his receptionist. He jammed his words together. "Gloria, get hold of my wife. Tell her to go home immediately and stay there. And, um,... and..."

"I'll find Angelique and tell her as well, sir," Gloria said carefully.

Rother grimaced. *See to your own first.* Your wife, your mistress. For a moment he hated his job and his career. He hated Hodges/Teague for putting him in this position. He hated whoever was being this latest terrorist attack. And he hated the frustration of helplessness.

Sutcliffe's eyes narrowed. "They'll activate security measures in the Flyover and Pacific time zones first, I imagine," he said. "In the meantime, the Chief of Staff will want reports from both of us regarding this... event. Let's make sure our statements agree, Colonel."

Dismissed, Rother stood up, saluted, and turned toward the door. His last thought before he left the office was, *You may be sure that my report will be factual, sir.*

⚯

French Lick, Indiana

Teague's B&Cs, although officially no longer accredited, got Kerise, Analou, and himself into Room 11 at the *Starbright Motel.* Maid service had yet to straighten and clean the room, which Kerise took as a good omen. The waste can beside the writing table contained an empty and crumpled bag of sour cream and onion potato chips, the wrappers from a couple of chocolate bars, an empty plastic soda bottle, and—perhaps best of all—two sheets of paper, wadded up.

While Kerise opened the papers, Teague located the remote and turned on the television set. The main channels all had "breaking news," and he selected CNN as the best of a dismal lot. The news was as bad as he had feared: explosions at fast-food restaurants all over the eastern seaboard. Death toll estimates in at least four figures; he thought they were highly optimistic. Evidently Rother had not been able to get Pentagon's G2 to make the necessary notifications—not that there had been much time in which to make them; still, perhaps they could save the other three time zones, at least to some extent.

Kerise placed a gentle hand on his shoulder. "I'm sorry, Teague."

He shrugged away without rejecting her sympathy. "You can only do so much," he whispered, his throat tight and dry. "What have you found?"

Before she could reply, Analou called out from the bathroom. "He's planning to come back."

Kerise met her at the doorway. "What makes you say that?"

Analou showed her the open medicine cabinet above the sink. "Shaving gear, toothbrush, toothpaste." She pointed to the curtain rod across the top of the shower stall. "Purple washcloth," she said, unnecessarily. "Not motel issue. The bar of bath soap in the dish is orange. Dial, perhaps. Certainly not the cheap samplers the motel provides." She lifted a pale eyebrow. "Did you check the closet and the drawers?"

"Not yet," answered Kerise. "Could you do something with an item of his clothing?"

Analou flashed her a scornful look. "What I can do is not Ouija-craft," she snarled. "It's not witchery, it's not—"

"I'm sorry," Kerise broke in. "I meant no—"

"I know you didn't. It's just that... you don't know. I mean, how could you know? Here, one example: a girl in one of my middle school classes tried to turn me in for—seriously—witchcraft, because instead of leaning over to pick up a pencil I had dropped, I simply brought it back up to my desk." She dragged a hand through her short yellow hair as they returned to the front room. "I suppose I can't blame her. Still, I finally had to shut it down whenever I wasn't alone. I didn't know what, or who, I was. Not until the Army tests. I figured it out."

"Teague?" said Kerise.

He was still staring at the television set. He stood at rigid attention, head inclined slightly so that he might confront the screen. "I can't watch this," he muttered, although he made no move to change channels or to turn off the set.

Kerise knew better than to touch him. Despite the intervening years since the World Trade Center went down, he remained inconsolable. He wanted no sympathy, no clucking sounds of pity, no solicitude. He wanted revenge. Only that drove him. She sometimes wondered whether he relished the pain he felt when he heard about terrorist attacks, as if he were somehow feeding on the horrors that were inflicted.

She also wondered, not for the first time, what arrangement her father had made with Teague to bind him to instructions. The Teague she had come to know was occasionally contrary, but he had served her well, and her father, too. But what could have been offered to Teague that would garner obedience from such an independent man? It had to be big, enormous.

She shuddered. Perhaps it was best that she did not know the terms and conditions.

Teague pressed the power button on the remote. In almost the same moment, the air alongside the bed began to shimmer. A moment later, Matthew Porter emerged into view.

Bladensburg, Maryland

The news regarding the explosions along the eastern seaboard brought Geneva Hartland's coffee mug to a stop halfway to her lips. A few drops sloshed onto her desk, just missing the keyboard. Her first thought was that Matthew Porter had something to do with them. But it soon became apparent, as she watched the live news feed on her computer, that the event was far too massive for one disgruntled paranormal psycho.

Her attention was so riveted that she did not realize Oliver West had entered the office until he was standing in front of her desk. Had he knocked, she wondered, but cast aside her irritation. Instead, she glowered at him and gestured him to silence. To compensate for his arrival, she raised the volume on the speaker.

"...in New York City. While no official estimates of injured so far, sources speaking on conditions of anonymity suggest that the figure will be in the tens of thousands. The highest casualties and worst damages occurred at those restaurants where parking spaces are located right up next to the building itself."

"Jesus," gasped West. "It's far worse than I first thought."

Hartland frowned up at him. "What did you first think, Oliver?"

He looked bewildered. "I don't know... two or three restaurants, maybe. Half a dozen. But certainly nothing on this scale of magnitude." He gathered himself, and shoved his hands into the pockets of his trousers, and sat down without invitation. "Could it be Teague?" he asked her.

Hartland considered this. "Based on what I've read about him, he would go after the Federal Government in some way," she said slowly, more musing than speaking. "He has done so on several occasions, although not with loss of life... yet. But the one act absent from his considerable resume is harm or death to innocent civilians. He hasn't stooped that low... yet."

"But he could," West pressed.

"I suppose so." Slowly she shook her head. "But not on this scale. And I feel that if even he did so, he would have a reason. It might not be a reason you or I would understand, but a legitimate one to him nonetheless. No, it takes a special kind of sick, degenerate, perverted mind to conceive and carry out a slaughter of this magnitude. This is simply mass murder, Oliver. And I fear it has only begun."

She sat back, her face grim. "That Somerville woman," she went on. "Didn't she show an innate ability to sense this sort of mind? And the telekine, Porter. Properly trained, he might defuse a bomb with his mind alone, or transfer it where it might detonate without harm, such as a desert, or the bottom of the ocean. Oliver, we may have been going about this all wrong."

Grumbling to West, she got out the scrambled and secure smart phone and initialized it. "As it's Sunday, I hope he's not out playing golf."

West raised both eyebrows. "With all this going on?"

"Oliver, golf is for obsessive-compulsives and anal-retentives. If Adrian were bitten by a rattlesnake on the third hole, he'd ask the quartets ahead of him to let him play through." She glared at the phone as if it were a rattlesnake. "Damn! I'll wager he left it on his armoir, not wanting to be disturbed while he five-putted a par three."

She clacked the phone down. "Oliver," she said, in a hard voice that surprised even her. "Find Adrian Dunbar and have him get in touch with me immediately. Tell him the action word is now Abort. He'll want to hear that from me, of course, but he may want to get that recall started. It looks like we may need Porter and Somerville after all, despite the risk they pose."

016

French Lick, Indiana

"Please wait," cried Kerise.

Matt said nothing while he surveyed the room's occupants. Teague was positioned to block access to the front door, as futile as that would be. Kerise did not move except for a spreading of the hands, pearl-gray eyes imploring him to give her a chance. But he settled on Analou Somerville.

"You?" he asked.

"And some inductive reasoning," she answered.

Matt nodded, an absent gesture. A decision tore at him. He might depart at will; they were powerless to hold him. But should he?

"You actually came looking for me," he said.

A faint smile played with the corners of Kerise's mouth.

"As impossible as that task must have seemed to you," he went on.

"There was no other choice," Kerise told him. "We need you."

Teague spoke up. "Travel anywhere is going to be very difficult for a while," he said to her.

She inclined her head in acknowledgement, without looking back at him. "Matt?" she said.

He shook his head. "What's going on? You said travel. What's the problem?"

"You haven't heard?" asked Analou, stunned.

He folded his arms across his chest, and shifted his weight to his right leg, and glared at them expectantly.

"Teague?" said Kerise.

The big man explained in hard and crisp detail, embellishing nothing. When he had finished, Matt clutched at his stomach, and sat down on the bed. He churned inside—for the victims, but also for his own plans, which might be thwarted by these developments. Even as that thought occurred to him, he felt shallow for it. The victims mattered, he told himself, and forget your plans, at least for the moment.

Matt's throat felt clogged with dry gravel. "Any attribution?" he asked.

"Who do you think?" Teague said bitterly. "But we don't want to offend the ucking fenemy, do we?"

"Teague," Kerise said quietly. She sat down beside Matt, and took up his hand in hers. "What's going on now is terrible," she told him. "But events like these are going to continue to happen. Here, or somewhere else. We've reached a point where problems outnumber solutions. A sieve isn't much good against a flood."

"I know that," Matt snapped.

"So the question is," she continued, unperturbed, "is whether you'd rather wage a futile fight against this sort of life, or start a new life where what you have is what you build."

He turned his head to look at her through misty eyes. "You know you're not making any sense, right?"

She sighed. "I suppose not." She released his hand, and nuzzled her face against his shoulder. "Matt... this talent of yours. What are its limitations?"

He scowled. "What do you mean?"

"Like, where can you go?"

"Oh. I-I... anywhere I've been, I suppose. I have to have a clear picture of my destination, either from experience or from, say, a photograph, or a video. I can't just poof out; this isn't magic, what I do." He glanced at her sharply. "Why?"

She took a step back, and did not answer directly. Her eyes, silver in the dim light of the motel room, took on a faraway look. "How much can you take with you when you go?" she asked.

Matt got up and stalked off, his shoulders rigid. "Oh, for God's sake," he grumbled. "Do you think I run tests to quantify the cargo? I've done tools. I've done a car, as you know. I've done..." He turned back around. "Never mind. What is it you're trying to find out, Kerise?"

She shook her head sadly. "It would do me no good to tell you, Matt. I *have to show* you."

He reached out for her. "Take my hand."

Her brow knotted. "Why?"

"I have something to show you. Take it."

She did. Dark nothingness enveloped them, then morning light and humid air.

⸻

Munich, Germany

Langford, already on edge due to the pistol in Sylvie's hand, cautiously opened the door. A uniformed porter stood in the hallway, a brown travel bag dangling by a strap from his right hand. His frown of puzzlement changed to a polite smile when Sylvie emerged into view, her right hand behind her. She accepted the bag with her left hand while Langford rendered a gratuity and breathed a little sigh of relief before closing the door.

"I didn't realize the Renauds were so dangerous," he said, with a gesture toward her back.

Sylvie cast the bag onto the bed and unzipped it. "It is that someone has gone to much of the trouble to prevent the information on the flash drive from becoming known too soon. Such trouble in my experience has been worth the lives." Poking through the items in the bag, she made a face. "I had not the plans for the prolonged stay," she groused. *"J'ai besoin plus des vêtements. Et je dors nue."*

Langford, who understood, struggled to find a response to the revelation that she slept in the raw. Finally he went to his own suitcase and dug out a triple-X large white tee shirt, which he held open to her. "Perhaps this will serve?" he asked.

Behind the tinted glasses, her eyes seemed to be smiling at him as she reached for it. *"C'est très gentil à toi,"* she said gently. "But I must still buy the brush and the tooth cream."

"Just the brush," Langford replied.

A moment stopped while they gazed at each other. Langford's heart thumped, and he wondered whether she could hear it. There were things that might be said in such a moment, but the only words he could think of were corny. He found himself wondering whether silence might be the best option.

Sylvie's lips glistened in the overhead light. Her words

80

allowed him to escape. "And the service room?" she asked.

Langford strangled a laugh. "Room service."

"Ah, *oui*, the room service. *Mais je n'ai pas faim.* I have not the hunger. I am tired; the traveling." She held the tee shirt against her, assessing her look. "It is that I should try this on, I think," she said, and went into the bathroom, closing the door behind her.

What, wondered Langford, *am I doing?*

Sylvie gave him only three minutes or so to answer the question. She emerged wearing the tee shirt, its length on her decent by about four inches. Quite clearly the garment contained only Sylvie. She spread her arms, inviting comment.

"It looks better on you," said Langford.

"I think perhaps I should—" she began, before the knock at the door interrupted her.

Langford, who was standing within arm's reach of the knob, opened the door without thinking. A burly man with a small pistol almost hidden in his thick hand stepped into the room, backing Langford off. He closed the door silently behind him.

On the east coast of Sri Lanka, northwest of Trincomalee

The sun was a red globe embedded in an eastern horizon smeared with pink and maroon. The colors marked the boundary between ocean and sky. Only a moment ago, that same sun had barely begun its western descent. Kerise's head swam. Matt steadied her.

"Where are we?" she asked. "Or *when* are we?"

He told her, adding, "It's early Monday morning."

She took a step on the white sand, and another. "Can you, you know, time travel?"

"If I could," he said tersely, "don't you think I would have?"

"Of course. Your brother. I'm sorry."

A hundred meters inland, a village of rudimentary huts lodged in the periphery of a vast and verdant forest. A few of the huts had suffered wind damage at some time in the near past. Thatch roofs spread askew, drooping over the frames of the walls. Trees rested where they had broken and fallen. Smoke rose from several of the huts; food preparation had already begun. Kerise caught a faint whiff of fish.

"A mail carrier from Trincomalee makes a weekly trip here," Matt explained. He stepped alongside her, blocking her as she began to drift up toward the village. "No, don't go any closer, not just yet." He pointed to an outcrop of dark rock, worn smooth by millennia of waves. "Let's sit over there."

Suddenly Kerise understood. *"Kinderheim,"* she said. "Manorema—the girl you sponsor."

"She just turned fourteen. They'll marry her off before the year is out. Or they might sell her. I don't know." He sat down, and slumped. "I keep telling myself that I can't catch all the birds that fall out of nests. But I thought... I thought I could catch this one. I've caught her for two years now. But I can't... can't..."

Kerise touched his shoulder. "You're thinking of swooping in and taking her away with you."

"So well you know me."

"You hesitate, because you don't know what you would do with her."

He looked away, toward the ocean, a wistful look in his eyes. "Yeah. That, and wondering whether I even have the right. Whether that's what she would want."

"In moral dilemmas, you do what you think is right, and do the best you can with it."

"Her father and a sister were killed in a cyclone that struck here last year," he told her. "As you can see, they haven't even begun to repair the damage. There's just no money, and the government is broke. Inflation is worsening. The mother's hands are warped with arthritis, yet she picks tea leaves for five hundred rupees a week."

"How much is that?" asked Kerise.

"About two and a half dollars. Marrying off Rema will free up a little more food for her brother and two sisters." His chest rose and fell with a wave curling. "I know it goes on like that, all over the world. In Thailand, men sink up to their knees in mud while they sift it for rubies for twelve hours, for less than a dollar a day. You'd think De Beers could afford a bit more."

"I think De Beers is mostly diamonds."

"Whatever."

"And you brought me here because—"

Abruptly he pointed. "There she is."

A tallish slender girl in a dark blue camisole and pale blue sari was walking along the edge of the beach toward the northwest, along with two other girls. She had long black hair bound in a tail that a mild breeze blew over her left shoulder.

"Dancer's legs," observed Kerise.

"I suppose so."

"You said she does traditional dance."

Despondent, he made a face. "Yeah, I suppose I did. Kerise... I brought you here because I wanted you to see what is important to me. There are things that I do, and that I will do, I have to do. I have no interest in your project, whatever it may be." He made a tiny, helpless gesture. "I'm sorry, but there it is."

"Matt...what if I could show you a place where she would be able to make her own decisions?"

"Seriously."

She flicked a smile at him. "I'd tell you that I would never lie to you, except that people who say that are usually on the verge of lying to you."

He gave a light laugh. "I see the problem. What did you want to say?"

"Come with me."

Matt stood up. "Damn it, Kerise, don't you *get* it?" He ticked points on his fingers. "One, I have my own agenda; it does not concern you. Two, I don't have the *time* to go around and around with you. Two, even if you told me—"

"Three."

He stopped. "What?"

"That's three, not two."

"Three?"

"So go on."

Chagrined, he turned toward the waves. "I-I forgot what I was going to say."

She got up to stand close beside him. It took an effort for her not to touch him, to lean against him. To slip an arm around him in affectionate support. "One day," she whispered, just above the hiss of the waves dying on shore. "That's all I'm asking for. If, after that day, you decide this isn't for you, then go your way, Matt. My not seeing you anymore will... well, perhaps it doesn't matter, in the long run. But please, just give me a day."

Matt jammed his hands in his pockets and gazed down at the sand at his feet. Kerise read this as a sign of imminent surrender, and waited patiently, her hand on the Palmetto in the back pocket of her black denims. Only the shallow movements of his chest indicated that he was even alive. She wished she knew what he was thinking, and whether she might help him resolve his obvious conflict.

At last he turned to her. The move brought them within a hand's-breadth of one another. She wondered whether he could hear her heartbeat, could see it pounding under the thin aqua tank top she was wearing. Suddenly she lost interest in his response. Placing her hands on his chest, she leaned forward and kissed him. He did not object or withdraw as the contact lingered. He tasted of yesterday's coffee and this morning's motel complimentary breath mint. The tip of her tongue caressed his lower lip. She pulled away.

"Right here. Right now," she breathed. "Anywhere. Whenever."

He frowned, and looked away. "I just don't get it."

"I just promised you, you would."

"No, I mean... I mean why? You don't even know me."

"I know most of the facts on record," she reminded him. "From them, I know that you can help us. Right here, right now, even that doesn't matter to me." She closed on him again. "I'd much rather spend that day in your arms, listening to the waves and the breeze and whatever birds there are here. You're right: I don't know all of you. I know enough. My feelings and my mind both tell me that. You are frustrating, conflicted, generous, compassionate, complex... and not all that bad-looking."

He laughed, despite himself. "What I have to do," he said, "I want to get over with. But it can wait. One day, Kerise."

She pulled out the Palmetto and brought up an image, which she displayed for him.

"Take me there," she said.

017

Munich, Germany

Langford had no choice but to look to Sylvie for cues. He had little doubt that she was able to deal with the circumstances, but what form her response might take, especially with himself much closer to the intruder, was beyond any live experience. Anything that he'd seen on television would probably get him and Sylvie killed. Still, the man had uttered no threats, and aside from barging into the room had made no hostile moves.

An inch or so taller than Langford, he outweighed the reporter by a good fifty pounds, and looked fit. His attire marked him as American: dark trousers with the cuffs well above the heels; a thin gray cotton shirt, without a collar and with a pocket, over a white tee shirt; and, of all things, Reeboks. He had shaved earlier that week, and his dark brown, windblown hair suggested work outdoors, as did his ruddy tan. From what Langford could see of the man's hands, they were hard but with trimmed nails.

Langford probed tentatively. "What do you want?"

"You've done something very foolish," said the burly man. As befit his size, he spoke with a gruff, authoritarian tone. "The only question now is: have you made any copies."

"No," he answered.

Sylvie merely shook her head.

"What's on it?" asked Langford.

The man shrugged. "No idea."

"Don't you even want to know?"

"I'm being paid to sanitize. That means retrieving the flash drive."

"And us," Langford said dully.

"You know it's something big. You know the date. You'll talk about it. Now, where is it?"

Langford started to turn. "It's—"

The man raised the pistol. "Ah-ah. Hands in the air, first." He glanced at Sylvie. "You, too, lady."

Sylvie's raised hands lifted the tee shirt well past her hips. For just a moment the burly man stared at her coal-black ruff. It was time enough for Langford to grab the pistol. Initially he managed to keep the short barrel away from him, but it was a losing battle. The man was too strong. He was trying to figure out something else to do when a bare heel slammed into the bridge of the man's nose. Bones cracked. His head was driven back, and he fell to the floor, his grip on the pistol now slackened.

Sylvie landed lightly on her other foot, and dropped to one knee on the man's groin. His body made no response. She leaned over him to look down into his face. She started to speak, then realized the futility of words. Presently the man's brown eyes dulled to old chocolate. She covered them with her hand, drawing down the eyelids. A huge breath steadied her.

Langford helped her back to her feet. A nebula of faint musk enveloped him—of exertion and a mild perfume. He fought it as she leaned against him for support.

"Thank you," she said, heavily accented.

"What," he wheezed, "is on that drive?"

They moved to the stuffed chair, where he sat her down. "It is the body of which must be disposed." She grimaced. "Tchah! It is to speak the English which I have lost."

"Take some breaths," he said. "I'll call Montclair. Maybe he's still in Munich."

That alerted her. "*Mais non*! You do not know how."

"I have his number."

"*Oui*. But it is this you must say."

At her instructions, he raised Montclair on the Palmetto. The conversation was amicable and quick.

"Something so soon?" asked Montclair.

"We just spoke with Veronique. She wasn't much help."

"Sorry to hear that. They just called my plane. I have to go. *Ciao*."

"*Ciao*," said Langford, to a dead link.

⁓⸻⁓

Northwest Brazil

Matt tugged at his jersey. "It's hot," was his initial assessment of their location. Already beads of sweat trickled down his forehead.

Kerise's tank top was darker in places. "We have A/C," she told him, and took his hand.

"What about Analou and Teague?"

"He'll remain where he was for two days," she replied. "Or until it's not safe, in which case he'll make contact with me. Stop worrying."

He sniffed. "There's smoke in the air. What's burning?"

"Brazil."

That stunned him. "In God's name, why?"

"The population of Brazil has more than tripled in the past three decades," she replied. "They need more arable land, so they're burning, or allowing to burn, the tropical forests. Indigenous peoples are being assimilated or eliminated. The fires are impacting global climate change far more than automobile emissions." She heaved a weary sigh. "Yet another reason for Indigo."

No one seemed to notice their abrupt arrival near the cluster of trees in the photograph she had shown him. Kerise leading, they passed through an open-air market ripe with the heady aromas of dead fish, hot spices, old sweat, and fresh fruit. On the other side of it waited a land rover. They climbed aboard, with Kerise driving. A few minutes later they left the town for a road worn through the forest by critters, carts, and the odd car that was sound enough to deal with the ruts. Kerise held loosely to the road, giving the land rover its head as she might a horse, nudging it back on track when necessary. Leaves and branches scratched at the frame, and occasionally left a mark on Matt's left arm.

"We had some brought over from England," Kerise explained, in response to his question about the vehicle. "It's easier to import parts, if we need them, than to rely on Brazilian dealers."

"But why Brazil?"

"Less hostility than Zaire or Angola, which were the other two options."

Frustration edged his voice. "See, that's what I'm talking about. You're so vague."

"That's a Carly Simon song."

"That's vain."

"Right, *You're So Vain*. Matt... *eh bien*." She did not look at his while she drove. "We needed a place with a thick canopy, the better to conceal our activities from satellites and drones. Politically, Brazil is relatively stable, and as long as we're well away from indigenous peoples, we're left alone. Equatorial Africa has tropical forests, but it's a land ruled by petty warlords, and the cost of graft and corruption would have been prohibitive, even for my father. At the moment, concealment is our best defense. So far, the Brazilian government does not know we're here. By the time they find out, we'll be gone. We hope to be gone."

"That's helpful," Matt snorted. He still had no idea what she was talking about. And her day was already an hour gone.

They crossed a river over a rickety wooden bridge. Matt held on tightly to the door frame and his seat.

"Relax," said Kerise. "One of the first things we did was shore it up. Small trucks can cross it. We haven't tried a semi yet... and won't; too much attention."

"Mysteriouser and mysteriouser."

"Follow the white rabbit."

He tried to find the sky through the foliage, and failed. "What do you do when it rains?" he asked.

"We get wet."

He lifted the hem of his jersey to wipe his forehead. "You mean wetter," he said.

"Sometimes I take a shower in it."

"That, I can't wait to see."

She grinned. "Actually, we're well underground, with a reinforced roof. Rain never reaches us."

She turned onto a side trail. After a few hundred yards, they came upon a pair of armed men in casual garb, and stopped. One of them stepped to the right side of the land rover and peered down at Kerise. Recognition was immediate: he snapped to attention, and waved her on.

"Those are Kalashnikovs," said Matt, after they had passed.

"You use what's readily available," replied Kerise. "We

got a good deal on a shipment of them from Kazakhstan, no questions asked."

"Jeez. Who *are* you?"

"Ah. Here we are."

They had reached a small clearing. Above them, over-hanging branches and fronds obstructed a view of the sky, but here and there were dollops of azure. Rays of sunlight streamed down onto the vehicle and onto Kerise's face. The *chiaroscuro* gave her a serene look that Matt found enchanting when combined with the mystery of her, and for a few moments he lost himself with her. Then she was getting out of the vehicle and stepping to a great tree. He watched, fascinated, while she opened a small door in the tree trunk to reveal an array of buttons and a keypad. She coded something—he could not make out what it was—and a great door, larger than that of a double garage, slid open on the ground, taking the surface of the terrain with it.

Kerise closed the tree door and returned to the rover, to drive it down the ramp in the hole. After they reached the next level, the door automatically closed over them, and lights came on.

They had reached a chamber walled in what appeared to be reinforced concrete. Ahead of them stood a divided metal door. Kerised touched a small keypad on the land rover, and the halves slid open soundlessly to reveal an elevator. She drove the vehicle in and closed the door behind them.

At another touch of the keypad, the floor began to descend. Matt shifted in his seat, now concerned for his safety even though there was no threat apparent. The walls of the shaft also appeared to be made of metal—like any other elevator, he thought. He reached out to touch the surface. His hand shook with the realization that the wall was not made of metal, but of some material that felt much like plastic.

"Structural plastic," Kerise explained. "Stronger and more durable than any metal or metal alloy. My father's creation," she added proudly. "Well, one of them, anyway. He calls it duranite."

"He must have gotten rich from this," observed Matt.

"Not one Euro—which I wish were francs. A country's money speaks of its history and culture. The Euro suppresses that, denies all that. My father calls it an unspeakable evil, and I agree. No, this plastic is not available on the open market. He began making his fortune in the aircraft industry. The new Mirage 5000 from Dassault-Breguet is based on his concept, although the Israelis have bought more of them than the French government. After he left Dassault, he took on consultation work, and was well-paid—for example, by the Saudis for advice on which aircraft to purchase to defend themselves against Iran. He has stock holdings in Silicon Valley and in China. Very diversified sources of income."

"I'd think that would gain a lot of attention," said Matt.

The elevator stopped. Another divided door opened to reveal a motor pool. Matt caught strong whiffs of petroleum products. Somewhere inside, someone dropped a wrench. The clanking echoed throughout the bay.

"We bank out of the Caymans," replied Kerise, as she climbed out of the vehicle. "And Switzerland, although we're very careful there. The Swiss are starting to cave against their privacy policies. A lot of despotic monies pass through there, most of it from Africa and eastern Asia, courtesy of American foreign aid, and the World Bank is finally putting a lot of pressure on them." She paused, waiting for him. "Coming?"

"You brought me all this way just to see a vehicle maintenance showroom?" he said, half-complaining as he got out. "I'm impressed by the subterranean facility, but now I have absolutely no idea what you could possibly need me for."

Kerise shrugged. "Someone has to watch me shower in the rain," she said lightly. "And wash my back. You're my only choice."

He rolled his eyes. She took his hand.

"Come with me," she said.

She led him to a simple door that opened on hinges, and they stepped through. On the other side, a corridor led past a few other doors on each side and terminated in yet another door. This gave onto a catwalk that extended all the way around an oval cavity a hundred meters across at its widest and whose depth Matt could not determine. But it was the great object in the cavity that riveted his attention.

"What is that?" he said, his voice suddenly hoarse. "Is that... nooo."

"Yes," said Kerise, matter-of-factly. "In common parlance, it's a spaceship."

018

Munich, Germany

It took Montclair ten minutes to return to Langford's hotel room. By that time, Sylvie had dressed, set the dead assailant in the stuffed chair, and brought a measure of calm to Langford with her soothing, accented voice. This was her kind of business, she told him. He had been afraid; that was nothing to be ashamed of. He had shown courage; that pleased her. In the end, he settled to a seat on the bed to await developments.

A code passed through the door between Montclair and Sylvie, and she let him in, her hand on the butt of her pistol as a precaution. Briefly she explained what had transpired, and how, in clinical detail. In her business, techniques and luck mattered. If a flash of pubic ruff causes a useful distraction, so be it.

"That was extremely dangerous," said Montclair to Langford, after Sylvie finished her report. "Amateurs get themselves killed trying to wrest a weapon away from a killer."

"I had to do *something*," Langford protested.

"And it worked out," agreed Montclair. "Just don't do it again."

"I don't want to have to do it again."

Montclair gave him a sharp glance, and turned back to Sylvie. "He was sterile?" he asked her.

"Not even the laundry mark."

"I don't recognize him," he said.

She shook her head, and showed him the photo she had taken on her Palmetto. "I have sent this to Interpol for the facial recognition," she told him. "I have not yet received the reply."

Montclair inspected the pistol. "Snub-nosed .32," he said, for Langford's benefit. "Good for close work, but still too much noise in a hotel like this. I don't think he wanted to kill you."

"He could have fooled me," griped Langford. "And allow

me to disagree: he said he was here to clean up, and that included Sylvie and me."

Sylvie nodded.

Montclair dashed out to the balcony and looked down. His hand smacked the railing; metal sang. "*Merde!*" he seethed.

Langford joined him, followed by Sylvie. "What is it?" he asked.

Montclair made a face at the avenue below. "He had help," he explained. "You were to be abducted and held incommunicado until that date. Whoever was driving has gone. He would have seen me enter, and know the game was over."

"That's two and a half months," said Langford.

"Then they will come here again," said Sylvie.

Montclair shook his head. "Probably not," he said. "They'll expect a trap now. Instead, they'll try to take you while you're on the street." He returned to the room and closed the sliding glass door behind them. "We have some options. One, remain here and live on room service. Two, place you in protective custody. Three, go about your lives, with tracers that will activate in the event of your abduction. And four, set up a trap on the street, where they might not expect one."

"The first two mean that you will do what they were going to do," Langford objected. "You'll put us on ice."

"*Qu'est-ce que c'est?*" asked Sylvie. "I do not do the skating."

Montclair explained curtly, in French.

Langford went on, "The last two could be combined into one, with the tracer as backup in the event of the trap failing to close."

Montclair nodded approval. "It seems you might have a little flair for this business."

"I hope not."

Bladensburg, Maryland

By early evening, Geneva Hartland had aborted the wetwork assignments that targeted Matthew Thomas

Porter and Anastasia Louise Somerville. Oliver West, the Chief of Security for Echelon, sat in a stuffed chair to one side of her desk, scarcely looking at her while she completed the last of her communications. The few glimpses he had taken left him with the impression that she was, in a word, frazzled. Several strands of her graying hair, normally in a tight bun, had come loose, somehow making her appear older than her age. Wrinkles around her eyes became more prominent. Her nostrils flared while she was speaking into the phone. West had never noticed this before. Pressure and stress did not become her.

Uncertainty began to set in for West. Her reversals of decision hinted to him that she might well hang him or anyone else in Echelon out to dry if it meant salvaging her career. As Chief of Security, he had the responsibility, regardless of Hartland's position, to guard the secrets of the unit, including those activities that should not see the light of day. Especially those.

He began to look at her with coldly professional eyes. In the wake of the restaurant bombings, the country now had other security concerns. Always too late to prevent attacks, the United States was now compelled to seal up even tighter than it did after the mass murders on 11 September 2001. Not only had Hartland cancelled the orders, she had imposed fresh ones: at all costs, locate and detain Porter and Somerville. West had no doubt that in the back of her mind lurked a notion that the two fugitives could be compelled to apply their paranormal talents to the defense of the nation. As to that, West had his doubts.

He had been involved with Echelon from its inception as a top secret effort by HomeSec to develop both weaponry and means of population control by subliminal forces. The identity of the population to be controlled had not been established or even questioned, which led West to believe the program was meant for local action. Philosophically the concept did not bother him; the media and social media were already hard on the job. But West envisioned abuse of the powers of paranormals for personal aggrandizement—few elected or appointed officials were able to rise above that. West even had doubts about himself.

And certainly about Geneva Hartland.

"You're pensive," she said, breaking up his thoughts.

His Palmetto gave him no time to respond. He glanced at it, then stared. His finger swept the screen to reveal the instant message. After he read it, he had to swallow to regain his voice.

"We may have caught a break," he told Hartland. "Teague has been spotted at the Starlight Motel in French Lick, Indiana."

Hartland's blue eyes gleamed. Passion filled her voice. "If he's there, Porter and Somerville could be there. I want all three of them alive. Get it in motion, Oliver."

He stood up. "Teague alive, too?"

Her hands made little shooing motions. "Of course, alive," she said peevishly. "If he's involved with the paras in some way, we need to know how. We can't interrogate him if he's dead."

<hr>

Northwest Brazil

Porter could scarcely contain himself. Amazement and irritation vied for control of his emotions, and neither won. But the latter drove his first words.

"*This* is what you wanted me to see?"

"Matt, you sound disappointed."

He whirled on her. "This has *nothing* to do with me. It cannot possibly have anything to do with me." He looked at it again. "Does it even work?" he asked.

"No," replied Kerise. "Well, yes, but... no."

"No more games, damn it!"

Her hand caressed his arm. Her tone was meant to soothe him. "You gave me a day. I still have a few hours."

"Not anymore."

"Please," she implored, breathless. "Please, Matt."

His eyes found hers, found a glint of silver in them. Straight yet pert nose amid a dusting of freckles. Thin lips, the tip of her tongue moistening them—not a sensuous act, but to lubricate her next words.

"We're leaving," she said.

"We?"

"Hush. I'll explain." She leaned on the catwalk railing, and he with her. "Earth is finished. It's had a taste of space, and abandoned it, satisfied with satellites and missile launch pads. Perhaps it will return to the Moon; if so, the purpose will be to develop a weapons platform from which to control the planet. Talk of going to Mars is just that: talk. The planet has billions of mouths to feed so that they can produce more billions of mouths to feed. People have become as locusts, consuming resources without doing anything with them. Space travel, to them, is a waste of those resources that could be better spent in feeding them. Earth is trading the stars for the mire. It is a horrible trade." She paused to catch her breath. "Even so, that's well into the future. We want, we hope desperately, to be long gone by then."

"You hope."

She nodded slowly. "Even paring down the load to the people and the essentials for a ten-year journey to Alpha Centauri, the amount of fuel we would consume during launch is prohibitive. We need FTL, and we are stymied."

He blinked at the acronym.

"Faster-than-light," she clarified.

"Ah. Of course. Can that even be done?"

She hesitated, and hedged. "We've made some progress," she said. "Not nearly enough."

"But what's that to do with me—" Abruptly he backed away, throwing up his hands. "Oh, no. No, no. No no no."

Kerise did not move. "Matt, there's simply no other way."

"I told you: I have things to do."

"So have I." She followed him as he backed along the catwalk. "And I can offer you something that Earth cannot possibly offer. Manorema Kulasingam; Miguel Dario; Veronique Ladama. The children you sponsor through *Kinderheim* can come with us. My father has already approved of this."

"Damn you," Matt seethed, halting. "You would use those I love against me?"

As he started to teleport himself to Columbus, her plea found its way through the haze of his anger—a simple,

"Matt, you promised me a hearing."

He pounded his fist on the railing, and hurt his hand. She took it up in hers and kissed it. He snatched it away.

"Matt."

His chest shuddered with the effort to calm himself. The warmth of emotion in his face began to fade. Now when he looked at her, the attraction of her eyes and her freckles meant nothing to him. She was the enemy, holding his children to be ransomed by his innate talent. But he had promised, as she reminded him. He would not sink to her level by breaking it.

"I can't take you to a place I've never been or seen," he pointed out.

"You've seen the Moon," she countered. "All you have to do is get the *Indigo* out into space."

A quick shake of his head rejected this. "I can move small household objects," he said. "Even a vehicle. *That*," he pointed at the spaceship, "is like an aircraft carrier."

"There is no paranormal difference between a plastic model X-wing fighter and a real X-wing fighter."

He rolled his eyes. "That is so *Star Wars*, Yoda."

"I concede that I don't actually know this. I just made it up."

He looked back down at the spaceship. "So this is the Indigo Project you spoke of."

She leaned on arms folded along the top of the railing. Half an arm's length away, he felt warmth emanate from her, and found himself wondering whether it stemmed from her work or from her stated feelings toward him. The thought softened his will and his annoyance. In that moment, she had ceased being his enemy. But what was she now?

"Why Indigo?" he asked.

She did not look at him as she spoke, but addressed the ship. "It's the prismatic color between blue and violet," she told him. "A few people, perhaps one in a hundred, can just make out a seventh color, indigo, between the two. It's there, but most can't see it."

"I think I understand."

"The governments of Earth would try to stop us, and damn the cost, if they learned what we intend to do. Matt, you know that."

He sighed. "Yeah."

"But," she said, reading his mood.

"Yeah. Kerise, I-I can't. Not now. Perhaps not ever."

She spoke as if she had not heard. "As for finding another world... Matt, you said you could go to a place you've seen. You even demonstrated that when you brought us here. You could take us to Alpha Centauri—"

"No, I can't."

"*Pourquoi*?"

He considered the question. At last he said, "Take for example the Red Spot of Jupiter. I could take you to it, I suppose, but it would do no good. Forget that we would die almost immediately upon arrival. The photo on which I based the journey was taken from, say, a hundred thousand kilometers above the Red Spot. Well, *that* is where we would wind up: the location from which the photo was taken."

"The *apparent* location," she amended.

"I'm not getting you."

"*Eh bien*. If I showed you a photograph of the Red Spot taken from the Hubble Telescope, you could take me to the apparent position from which the photo was taken." He nodded, and she went on, "In the same way, the various high-resolution telescopes now in orbit have taken photographs of many worlds in disk form. You could take us to the apparent positions for them."

"That could still be light-years," he argued.

"Even so, once we reached that position, you would be able to see the disk, and take us directly there."

Still he objected. "To what is probably an uninhabitable gas giant."

"*D'ac*," she said, the curt French startling him. "But there would be other worlds in that system. And the giant itself might have habitable moons. *Par example*, consider our Ganymede and Callisto."

"You lapse into French when you become animated."

"A shortcoming that prevents me from being perfect."

"Kerise—"

She took his hand. "Come with me."

Reluctantly he yielded. "Where?

"To my room."

019

French Lick, Indiana

Teague peered around the side of the curtains without moving them. "What is it?" asked Analou.

He pulled back. "Nothing."

"Your heart rate is up, your adrenalin is up, the muscles of your shoulders are knotting, your hand is on your sidearm, and there's something black out there," she said. "Would you care to run that response by me once again?"

"Right. You're the telempath."

Analou sat down on the bed and bounced a couple of times. "I loathe that term."

"What would you call it?"

"I'm not sure there is a word for it."

He threw a sharp glance at her before returning to the window. "You said something was black out there. What does that mean, exactly?"

She made a little sound of annoyance. "I don't know," she complained. "I haven't figure this all out. I sense things, okay? Someone or something in the area has evil intentions. I can't be any more specific than that, okay?"

"In the area?"

"I don't *know*," she snapped. "Within a block, maybe."

"What else?"

"What do you mean, what else? There's nothing else."

"You described my physical condition," he reminded her. "How did you manage that?"

Her gaze shifted to the floor between her feet. "I-I... I got inside your mind a little. I wanted to know what was going on. I'm sorry."

Teague rubbed his chin thoughtfully. Her face twisted as she looked away. "Don't doubt yourself," he said at last. "Your abilities can help keep us alive."

"Matt and Kerise. Where did they go?"

"I'm not sure," he replied. "Go into the bathroom and see if you can get into the air vent."

Her face red, she got to her feet. Her question challenged him. "Is this a short joke?"

"They probably won't look for you there," he said smoothly. "I'll tell them you went with Porter."

"I don't understand."

"Right now my job is to protect you," he explained, with growing impatience. "They'll come for me. They don't know about you."

"But—"

"Just go look."

She put her hand to her forehead. "It hurts."

He turned back to her, an unspoken question on his face.

Tears formed in her eyes. "I've got them," she said, her voice feeble now. "I'm blocking them. Come with me. We can get out through the bathroom window."

"Blocking them?"

"They're confused. They're looking about, trying to figure out why they're where they are. Hurry!" she pleaded. "I can't hold them all for much longer."

***

Northwest Brazil

"You *have* been in a girl's room before," said Kerise.

Matt shrugged. "It's been a while."

It was a simple enough place—four sheet-rock walls, all painted chartreuse, a forest green ceiling, a thick aqua carpet on the floor. Enough space to move around without stepping on one another. One made-up twin bed with a plain brown comforter that did not quite fit the room's décor. A computer desk and a straight-backed cushioned chair. A metal clothes locker in one corner, a narrow blond dresser in another. A white cooler doubled as a night-stand.

No window. It was not a room for habitation, but a cell to retreat to. He told her as much.

"I have a couple *pieds-à-terre* elsewhere, not much different from this room." She sat down on the bed. "This will have to serve us as a sofa," she said, patting a spot beside her. "There are sodas and Evian in the cooler. I'd like an RC."

Matt hesitated, eyeing the bed suspiciously.

"I can think of several young men who would love to sit there," she chided. "Two or three older ones as well. But I have never issued but one invitation to my bed, and that just now."

"I'm noth—"

"Hush. The sodas?"

Again Matt considered whether simply to depart. Arguing with himself, he pointed out that in bringing Kerise to Brazil, he had in effect abandoned Analou to whatever fate befell Teague. Life might be tough and unfair, but he didn't have to be. Relenting, he grabbed the drinks and dropped down beside her, popping his open to a light spray. She reciprocated, her silver eyes laughing at him.

"It's a bit intimate," she said. "But it's all I have." She toasted him, and they drank. "Matt, I didn't bring you here to seduce you. Not that I'd mind, of course, but you are much more than who you present yourself to be." She held up a hand. "No, please don't say anything. Let me bring my case."

He grimaced, and nodded.

"I don't know how you see yourself," she went on. "I can guess at some of it. You have something dark that drives you away from me. In some way, you feel yourself unworthy... of me, I would like to think, but it's more than that. You feel a guilt you don't deserve—no, don't argue with me, please, because this is not an accusation, merely an observation.

"But you don't see yourself as I see you. A man who is generous with his very limited funds. Who has known joy and war and grief. Who means well; that's important to me. You're a good person, Matt, despite how you might feel about yourself. You matter to me. Yes, I've read dossiers and surveillance reports and background checks. They describe you. But they are dusty letters of dried ink on paper.

"I had been watching you for about nine days—I had trips to Suriname and to Germany to make before I could devote time to you. I would have watched you for longer, perhaps even contrived to meet you without alarming you, but events conspired to move our encounter forward, under circumstances I had hoped to avoid."

She paused, smiling at some memory.

"I was going to present myself as a sort of *femme fatale*, with a dark secret that I would gradually drag you into, to the point where you would be unable to extract yourself. You would want into Indigo, once you had been led very delicately to it. As much as I would have enjoyed using myself as bait, that was not the original plan. The kill order against you and Analou and Carlos Vega forced me to advance my timetable."

She picked up his hand and made him look at her. "Despite a few miscommunications and frustrations, being with you has confirmed for me what I already suspected. Matt... please, please, believe me when I tell you this, for it is independent of anything else I am doing: I love you."

He did not move, nor avert his eyes. He told himself that the revelation should not have stunned him, that he had known at some point it would come to this, and yet even in the confinement of her bedroom he was unprepared for it.

He was equally unprepared in his response. To him, she had the permanence of an impulse. He knew a lot about her and yet almost nothing. She had courage. She made glib remarks during dangerous moments. She possessed a competence that he could not begin to describe: she seemed to know what she was doing, even in unexpected circumstances. But who was she? Who the hell *was* she?

For a few moments he forgot his hatred, his anger. For a few moments, Jesse was no longer in his thoughts. He closed his eyes. If he could see an after-image of her face, the way one sees a bright light after looking at a light bulb... but what would that mean? And yes, there she was, with that tiny and mysterious smile just curling the corners of her mouth, as if she understood his quandary and was waiting for him to resolve it, one way or another.

Her eyes. Luminous gray, and in certain light they glowed as fresh silver. He could feel them on him. But was she asking herself who the hell was he? Or did she already know?

Her hand lightly on his thigh made his eyes open.

"Do you really think I can help you?" he asked, and immediately regretted the question, for it implied a form of surrender, that he was considering her offer.

Her hand gave him a little squeeze. "Don't you?"

"I suppose I could practice," he allowed. "Work my way up from delivery vans to oil tankers. Kerise... are conditions really so bad that you'd abandon everything and just leave? Without trying..."

"Trying what."

He could not answer.

"Matt, those conditions include the attacks today in the United States. There simply are too many problems."

"You've said that."

"*Oui.* I have. It's like that game with the hammer and the little creatures that pop up through openings in a board. You bash one back down, and another appears. And so on and so on, and you never ever get all of them bashed down at once. That's how it is, all over this planet. Do I truly need to spell it out for you in great detail? Can't you see what's going on? And it won't stop, Matt, *it will not stop.* It is now beyond repair. Hate is winning. It *has* won. Country against country, government against government, government against its own people, race against race, culture against culture, people deliberately set against one another by the media, by politicians in power or seeking power... *mon Dieu!*"

Breathing heavily, she shot to her feet and went to stand by the door, as if to leave. Her shoulders slumped. Her whisper barely reach him. "It is a curse, this gift of sight, of seeing what so many do not, cannot, or refuse to see. If more had the gift of vision, and the sense to see what could be done... then perhaps. *Peut-être. Mais, non.*"

Slowly she turned around.

"Do you know... I spent a year in public school in Seattle," she went on. "Fifth grade. My father was back and forth, negotiating some business with Boeing, and it was decided that my mother and I should remain there. I was given many tests, because my scores were so high, and the school received federal money. At the same time, I was belittled for my mind. I was too smart. It wasn't nice to show up the other students by knowing the answers." She spread her hands helplessly. "Matt, how do you fight something like that? How do you even begin to? And what sort of country would deliberately suppress the intellectual development of its best and brightest in order to salve the feelings of those who simply plodded along? It's national suicide by mys-education, Matt."

He patted the spot next to him. "Sit down," he said gently.

Laughing, she did so. "You're the only one I can do this with," she said.

"What's that?"

"What you call it, rant. I'm afraid, Matt. I see so much, yet I have so little power to effect change, to make a difference that's worth something. And I would not want that power. I have no right to impose my ideas or my beliefs on anyone else. They are mine, to share, *oui*, but not to crush."

She made a little movement with her hands, as if to take his, and finally settling for folding them onto her lap.

"So we, people like my father and I, we are leaving," she continued. "We are of similar minds, and yet varied, different. We sift to determine the best that we can do."

"And I'm the best you can do? Seriously."

"You are he whom I have chosen," she said simply, studying her hands. "I cannot tell you why that should be. I can only tell you that it is. My heart agrees with me."

He had no idea what to say to that. A moment passed in silence. He wanted to kiss her, but held back. To have touched her in any way would have been to accept what she was telling him, accept what she wanted. Instead, the ghost of Jesse called to him.

"I can't," he said.

"I know."

Her Palmetto sounded: a series of five reedy beeps—three followed by two. Air left her, and she hung her head.

"What is it?" asked Matt.

"Teague. That's one of the codes we developed. He's been taken."

020

The Pentagon

Lieutenant Colonel Albert Rother's fingers kept striking keys erroneously as he struggled to prepare the report of Teague's notification of terrorist activity and the response by the DCS for Intelligence. Response? The mere word elicited a bitter laugh from Rother. He had to look up the word "dawdle" to make sure he spelled it correctly. Irritation bordering on anger made him type it three times before he got it right.

Rother sat back. Coffee, he thought, and got up and went to the table by the window to pour himself another cup. The window gave on to the northeast, to Alexandria and the District. Even at this distance he could make out a few plumes of smoke.

Maybe the attacks on the East Coast could not have been prevented. Teague had only found out about them moments before the IEDs started to explode. The rogue agent had done the best he could under the circumstances, placing his very life at risk to warn Rother. His thoughts returned to the conference with General Sutcliffe, and the general's abrupt dismissal of him. Who, indeed, was the rogue here? Wasn't Intelligence supposed to *act* on reports, at the very least to determine their credibility? Well, subsequent events certainly had confirmed their credibility in this case.

Rother returned to his desk and flopped down in the castered chair. Coffee sloshed from his mug onto the carpet. He cursed; for good measure, he added an epithet against Sutcliffe. His eyes darted to the open door to see if anyone had overheard. But he was alone.

Well, so was Jeremiah.

He scrolled through what he had written, and made a few cosmetic changes—a word here and there, a missed punctuation. Gradually it sank in that his career was on the line. The report would go to the Chief of Staff of the Army, who was General Sutcliffe's immediate supervisor, and to the newspapers. One way or another, he thought, "the truth shall set you free." The death toll could be and probably was well into the thousands. He had followed procedures and guidelines. He had done almost all that he could. Almost. He still had to tell the truth.

He hit SEND, and waited for the shouting and the recriminations to begin.

French Lick, Indiana

A goddamn gopher hole.

They had been running across an open field and he had stepped in a gopher hole, and turned his left knee. By the time he was able to stand, he was the focus of five automatic pistols and an Uzi. The girl, at his insistence, had kept running; she was nowhere in sight. Teague had done that part of his job.

At least, he thought, Analou got away.

Hooded and with his wrists zipped behind him, he had been taken... somewhere. He estimated the length of the journey at eleven minutes and about four miles. The room in which he now sat smelled of old cigarettes, old sweat, and fresh coffee. He doubted the coffee was for him.

Around him he counted three different breathers. One of them had a hack as well—a smoker, likely. The smell of fear emanated from another. The respiration of the third sounded calm and measured. He was the one in charge.

The trio had several options open to them. They could commence an interrogation now, although he had no clear idea what they might want to know from him. They could wait for the arrival of higher authority—someone from Langley, he supposed, although that might be a long wait, with all flights grounded due to the terrorist attack. That he was hooded suggested they might keep him alive for a while, as their identities would be meaningless if he were dead. A simple maneuver to snap the plastic strip binding his wrists might save him, if and when push came to shove. In any event, he had nothing to do but await developments and learn as much as he could.

Surely a bit of conversation couldn't hurt. He said, "I

can only imagine what the motel manager thought when he learned that four men would be occupying a room with but one bed."

Teague heard a little puff of air. His jab had gotten to one of his captors. That sensitivity might prove useful later. A sharp intake of breath followed, and a not-unexpected question. "Where's the girl?"

The voice came from a little to his left. He turned his head to answer. "I don't know where she went." That much was true, although he doubted they would believe him. As they had yet to pound on him, he concluded that chemical interrogation might well be in the offing. Sodium pentathol was probably too much to hope for—he had been trained to defeat it. Still, even with an injection of Pravadex, he could reveal no more than that.

At least they had unwittingly told him that he was not the primary focus of their mission. The pursuit of Analou narrowed down their parent organization to just one: Echelon.

"So what now?" asked Teague.

Nobody answered. Someone to his right shifted on his feet, putting his weight on one leg. It dawned on Teague that the men were skittish. But why?

"Who's running Echelon these days?" he asked casually. "Hartland, right? Did she get manage to get a flight out of Langley, or is she driving?"

"Special clearance chopper."

Teague nodded to himself. So they were a little talkative. And with Hartland involved, it confirmed his estimate of Echelon.

"So the *grande dame* herself is coming," he mused aloud. "With all that's going on today, I wonder why she made me her top priority."

"Shut up."

"I'm a clam."

A brief silence, then a buffet across the top of the head. "Where's the girl?"

"Make up your mind," Teague replied. "Which is it?"

"The girl," said the same voice. "Anastasia Louise Somerville. She's wanted."

"She didn't mention that to me."

"There's no reason she should have, Teague."

This from a new voice, and Teague was just able to conceal his surprise. So there was a fourth person in the room. Male, older by the sound of the voice, and casually in charge.

"How did you come by that name?" the man asked. "A Company-assigned code name, is it?"

"I was posted to South Korea some years ago," Teague answered, readily enough. "The city of Taegu. It gradually morphed into a name for me, a point of reference. I kept it."

"This was before—"

"Yes," Teague said quickly.

"A memory of better days. But you're not working for the Company anymore. You transferred over to HomeSec, as I recall. Stole a bunch of Nine-Eleven documents and got yourself on a target list. Funny thing, though: the documents never turned up. All the acronyms thought you'd use them somehow. Sell them to Wikileaks, maybe. Imagine the damage those documents could do to our intelligence services if they were ever made public."

"Gomez," said Teague.

"I wondered when you'd get around to recognizing my voice."

Teague shook his head. "It wasn't that, although it helped. When you referred to the services as acronyms, that clinched it."

"So here we are."

"This isn't about those documents."

Gomez gave a light laugh. "I thought, as long as we're waiting. Hang on a tick."

Teague heard a faint snap of static. Gomez was receiving a transmission. Ever so slowly he began to tighten the zip at his wrists. With the right leverage, the right torque, he could snap the plastic like a toothpick. Yet surely his captors were aware of that. They themselves had been trained in the technique. Teague eased back.

You want *me to try to escape.*

But why?

Standing orders are to kill me on sight, he reasoned, so they don't need an excuse. They have to assume I would try to escape anyway, so the attempt is not unforeseen. So... they want Analou. They think I might lead them to her, and/or possibly to the documents. All of which means...

Which means they've placed a tracer somewhere on me.

⁂

Northwest Brazil

Kerise sipped at her coffee while she considered her response to Matt's query. They had repaired to what she called the Mess, a term of military origin. He had passed on coffee, opting instead for a soda. He sat opposite her at the table, seemingly attentive, but his eyes kept wandering. She hoped he was not considering a transfer, and abandon her here. With flights grounded, the U.S. might shoot down anything, however innocuous, that invaded their air space. She would have a difficult time tracking him down again.

"Teague knew the risks," she said, her voice just audible above the din of food preparation. "He's being well-paid to take them."

"Kerise," he said, his gaze now riveted to hers. "It's not a good idea."

"Why not?"

He sat back, stunned that she would ask.

"You're right," she said, miffed. "It was dumb. We don't know the situation on the ground, so to speak. We might transfer into a firefight, or worse. Sorry—I'm not thinking."

"So think."

The coffee had cooled enough for her to fortify herself with a gulp of it. "All right," she said. "With flights grounded, they won't have taken him very far. They'll hole up somewhere, probably still in French Lick, and call for instructions. Teague's signal meant that he had been taken, captured. They didn't kill him outright, despite standing   orders."

"They want something he knows," Matt put in.

Kerise felt her heart skip. "Analou."

"But that could work to our advantage."

111

She brightened. "You can take us directly to her."

"I can, yes."

"Will you?"

He traced a design with his fingertip in the condensation on the table top. He spoke without looking at her, as if he were addressing that design. "You have to understand, Kerise. Yes, what you propose to do here is interesting. But I have my own agenda, my own project. I have a... promise to keep."

"I wish I understood."

He folded his hands together and pressed his lips to them. She had no idea what he was thinking. His face was devoid of expression, his eyes closed as if to shut out pain. She would ease that for him, if she knew how. Her hand drifted of its own will across the table to grasp both of his. His eyes opened to her.

"Kerise," he whispered.

"Right here, Matt."

Weariness added a line to his forehead. "Finish your coffee."

She lifted the mug. "Why?"

"We can at least try to find Teague and Analou."

French Lick, Indiana

The opportunity for escape, when they presented it to Teague, was laughably easy. Two of the men went to dinner. A third went to the bathroom. Teague counted footsteps, and concluded there were two men in the bathroom. In seconds he was able to snap the zip strip confining his wrists, and to yank off the hood.

He was alone in the motel room. It was similar to, but not the same as, the room that had been let by Matthew Porter, and he realized he had been taken in a roundabout way back to the *Starbright* Motel. He got to his feet and knew that he had been sitting for too long. A few quick stretches restored his circulation. A moment later he was running in bright sunlight along a street trafficked mostly by semis. One roared past him, honking, as he cleared in front of it with just a few feet to spare. He dodged into the convenience store and asked for the rest room keys.

After locking himself in, he quickly stripped and felt up each item of clothing. Failing to find the trace, he ran his hands over his skin without encountering any unexpected lumps. It would not be very large—the size of a grain of Korean barley, perhaps. They wouldn't have implanted it in the traditional sense; a mere subdermal injection would have sufficed, like a tetanus shot. He checked his scalp again. There, just at the crown. Difficult to see in the mirror, because he would be forced to look down. The injection site would have healed over, but he still might treat the tiny lump as a zit.

Teague placed his thumbs carefully on either side of the lump. Pressed together, they folded skin, stretching the center taut. The sensation from his teenage years returned. The zit was about to yield. It yielded. He felt the trace land at the top of his forehead. Carefully he got it on the tip of a finger to examine.

The trace was a black dot attached to a drop of blood. He'd heard whispers of it here and there. The delivery principle was similar to that employed by the Russians against the Bulgarian defector Markov back in the Seventies; in this case, the trace might have been implanted by a powerful puff of air through a straw. Langley had played with the concept in the interim. He held up the device to the light and wondered what to do with it. He'd need a hammer or something equally solid to crush it and disable it. He peered into the toilet bowl. Let them chase sewage, he thought, and flicked it in, flushing after he did so.

He did not, however, believe that he had located all the traces. They'd implant one trace relatively easy to find, hoping he would ignore the possibility of a second one.

Or maybe they weren't that cunning. Most of the newer crops of agents had failed to impress him. Maybe they'd learn; maybe they'd die trying. It wasn't his concern any longer; neither was the trace he was unable to locate. He was still being paid to do a job.

He washed his hands and the top of his head, and walked out, returning the key before he left.

Gasping for breath, Anastasia Louise Somerville finished crossing the open field and ducked in front of a small strip mall along the street that fronted the field. She had not looked back at Teague. His terse command of flight brooked no argument. Moreover, her sensory perception detected the power behind his insistence; as much as she loathed abandoning him in this desperate moment, she "saw" that her obedience enabled him to perform the duties for which he had been paid. He knew what he was getting into; he knew what was likely to happen to him. His command bestowed upon her the best protection he could muster.

But darkness diminished with distance. The little prickles she had been feeling all along—some of them had to be caused by Teague. By what was inside his mind. He was acting heroically, yes. But he was also capable of terrible deeds, and in the time she had spent in his company, she had come to see that he was contemplating such a deed.

She turned around. panting. She had come to rest at the front of a salon. It was open, and invited walk-ins, and there was just one stylist within, a taller woman in shirt and slacks covered by a full blue apron. She was a blonde on this occasion—her black roots were already visible, despite the distortion of the window glass—and she had, Analou decided, a professional and sensitive aura.

After ascertaining that the salon was otherwise unoccupied, Analou stepped inside. To the question in the woman's brown eyes, she said, "Can you dye my hair?"

"Of course." Her name tag read "Renée." She motioned Analou to a rotational chair with a sink behind it. "What color would you like?"

Analou sat down. "As black as you can get it," she replied. "So black it has blue highlights."

Renée draped a cloth over Analou, and tied it snugly at the back of her neck. Presently she set a bottle on the work counter, tilted the chair back so that Analou's head and neck rested over the edge of the sink, and turned on the water. When it was warm enough, she began to wash and color Analou's hair.

"Just visiting?" she asked.

Analou started. Quickly she assessed Renée, and concluded that the question was innocent. She kept her tone friendly, and slightly amused. "What makes you say that?"

"Your tan," answered Renée. "That's not from an overhead lamp."

"I spend most of my time in the Southwest. But no, not visiting, just..."

"I didn't think so."

The declaration made Analou blink. She found herself debating whether to get out of the chair and leave.

Renée paused in the shampooing. "I'm sorry. That's none of my business. It's just that..."

"I seemed to be running from something?" Analou suggested.

"Well... yes." She resumed the sudsy scalp massage. "You're very observant."

Renée laughed. "This is French Lick, Indiana, home of Larry Bird... and not much else. Well, you looked furtive, and a little out of breath, and then you came in and asked for a change of appearance. I merely added two and two."

"You're very good at math."

"Hold still, I'm going to rinse."

"Me, or you?"

Again the stylist laughed. "Is that too hot?"

"Nice."

Analou squeezed her eyes tighter. Her mind reached out to Renée again. The woman was who she presented herself to be: observant, curious, competent, and slightly jaded. Nothing ever happened in a small town. Except when it did.

"Did you hear those two explosions earlier today?" Renée asked.

"Haven't you been watching TV?"

"I'm rarely *that* bored. Besides, there's no TV in here."

"I don't know all that much more," said Analou. "But my companion found one of the bombs, and disarmed it. He called it in to someone in Washington."

The spray moved off to one side. "Bombs?"

"In backpacks, old cars, shopping bags, and other innocuous containers that look as if they've been left behind. Things you might not notice, despite the 'See Something, Say Something' initiative. The Eastern Time Zone has been hit pretty badly."

The spray continued. "Terrorists?"

Analou managed to nod, despite the confinement on the sink. "They think my companion is responsible, but he actually saved a lot of lives today. They were chasing us... they caught him, but not before he got me away."

"I'm sorry."

"Me, too."

"What are you going to do? Here, let's sit you up... there. So what are you going to do?"

I'm going to rescue him, she thought. Aloud, she said, "I don't know."

Renée threw a towel over Analou's head and commenced to dry her hair. Suddenly she paused. "There's a man looking in the window," she said softly. "He looks official, and annoyed. He's coming in."

"Oh, Jeez..."

Slowly Renée continued to dry her hair. Analou withdrew inside herself and focused. Sensors detected the man in indescribable colors, like something seen through infrared filters, only hers were well beyond that portion of the electromagnetic spectrum. His silhouette showed up in relief against the inorganic background of the salon front. She detected sounds; he was speaking. She added the sounds to her focus.

"We're looking for a woman who may have run in here."

A woman was added to her focus, conjured from memory. Aunt Maude, whose hair color varied week by week from electric blue to shocking pink, and was now lemon yellow with myrtle green detailing. Wrinkles, a pug-like nose. Lips as if trying to recover from a rictus of perpetual disapproval.

"Let's see who you have under there."

Light rose from below as the towel was drawn away. Analou noted it and set it aside. The store and the man remained in nameless colors. She sensed a moment of shock. Gruff sounds.

"Pardon me, ma'am."

Darkness descended back into place. The silhouette floated into light, and then away. Behind her, Renée stumbled back. Analou sensed a new color, this one named: confusion.

Analou blinked, and took a deep breath. Her vision restored, she glanced over her shoulder. "It's okay," she soothed. A moment later, she added, "My hair is still damp."

"He looked right at you," gasped Renée.

"He was probably looking for someone else," Analou replied, with as much sincerity as she could muster.

"Maybe," Renée said, dubious. She recovered Analou's head with the towel. "I-I don't understand…"

"'There are more things in heaven and earth, than are dreamt of in your philosophy,'" quoted Analou.

Renée paused. "Hamlet," she said. "Act…one?"

Analou smiled under the towel. "Yes. So you know that one."

"I studied drama before I ran out of money," said Renée. "I got a small grant to attend a beauty school, which is how I wound up here."

"I don't know whether to be sorry or glad."

"Some cloud linings are lead, and others are silver."

Analou laughed. "I know just what you mean."

Renée pulled the towel away. "There. That's about as dry as I can get you without using a hair dryer. I'm thinking you're in a hurry. Here, let me comb it out a little, and make it look more presentable."

Five minutes later, Analou inserted her chipped card, and waited. After thirty seconds, the tiny screen read "unaccepted." She tried once more, to the same result.

"It looks like they've found you," said Renée.

"And they'll trace me here. I have some—"

Renée made little shooing motions. "Just go. You can pay me later."

"No, I have some cash." She drew a thin wallet from the front pocket of her jeans and peeled off a twenty and a ten. "No change, please," she said.

"I-I… Thank you…"

Analou met her eyes. "I won't forget this," she

promised, and walked out of the salon.

021

French Lick, Indiana

Geneva Hartland gradually came to the realization that if she did not resolve the question of the two remaining known paranormals one way or the other, she might as well forget submitting her resume elsewhere in the current administration. She might find employment as a consultant to one of the House Committees, especially if she did so quietly and without pushing the issue. A post at Georgetown University might suit her briefly, but she'd had only one year of teaching, two decades ago at Penn State, and hadn't liked it then, and doubted she would enjoy it now.

With Somerville missing and Teague wandering without apparent aim, she'd had nothing to do upon her arrival in French Lick. Now she was sitting outdoors in front of a small café, drinking a latte and debating whether to take up smoking once again. Pondering the unsolvable had rarely appealed to her, but in this instance she struggled to understand what had happened to a perfectly structured process of elimination. Echelon was in place at all three sites. They'd found and killed Carlos Vega, and pursued the other two without success, although they had managed to track one and locate and chase the other, both here in French Lick. What a godawful name for a small city. Doubtless the neighboring cities were German Belch and Mexican Fart. Even the latte tasted more of milk than of coffee.

Hartland drummed her fingers on the round white table, to the tune of metal singing. People passed in front of her, their glances incurious. Ordinary people, harmless. They had no idea what went on in the world, and couldn't care less to find out. Teleportation and telepathy were devices to make science fiction shows interesting. But if you could control the people who were gifted with such devices... there was no end to the possibilities. No one was immune. You could know what your opponents were thinking. You could have them swooped up and dropped off in Antarctica. You could *control* the country...the *world*!

She amended that thought, and not for the first time: *I myself* could control the country and the world. The possibility excited her heart, and not for the first time.

Along the far side of the street walked a stocky man who was completely bald. Hartland gave him no more than a passing glance before taking another sip of bad coffee. Without warning, two people appeared before him: a dark-haired man and a carroty-redheaded woman. Startled by realization, Hartland choked and coughed. She fumbled for her Palmetto, and dropped it on the concrete patio. It broke. She swore.

⸻

French Lick, Indiana

"Judas Priest!" yelled Teague. "Don't *do* that to me. I almost killed you, by instinct, by too long doing what I do. Don't ever do that—"

Kerise's hand over his mouth hushed him, but he shoved it away and glared at her.

"Where's Analou?" she asked.

Teague began to usher them around the corner of a store and into an alley. "She got away," he answered, recovering. "I was taken briefly. I think I have a tracer somewhere inside me. They're hoping I lead them to her. You'd best separate from me."

Kerise nodded. In the brief and concise reply he'd given her all he had, and wanted nothing more than to protect them by distance. He had the look of a man in a hurry to catch a bus. Gently she placed a hand on his chest. Physically she could not prevent him from doing whatever he wanted. Well aware of this, she opted for tenderness.

"Matt can get us all away from here at a second's notice," she whispered. "Now, we need to find Analou and get her away from here, too. So what arrangement did you make with her? Where did she go?"

Teague answered without hesitation. "She'll make her way to the car and wait there. She'll get into the trunk through the back seat if she sees anyone or anything suspicious."

"How long ago…"

"She's probably there already. Kerise, we can't take the plane. Flights are grounded. Even if one lifts off from Mexico, a drone will shoot it down."

She slipped an arm around each man, and nodded to Matt. Seconds later, they were standing at the side of the rental car in the parking lot where they had left it. In the front passenger seat, Analou jumped and yelped at their abrupt arrival. Relief slackened Kerise's shoulders as she beckoned to the telepath.

"Once more into the breach," she told Matt.

He grumbled something. Light passed, then darkness, then light, all changes taking place over a span of two or three seconds. Afternoon sun greeted them when they arrived at the Cessna in Chihuahua State. Jacques was waiting by the hatch as if he had expected them to arrive at just that moment, but Kerise paid scant attention to him. The ease with which Matt had conveyed them astonished her yet again. She thought she should have been used to this by now, she should have known what to expect. One knee felt as if it were about to give out. She put a hand against the fuselage to hold herself upright.

Teague's look was expressed in Matt's question. "Are you okay?"

In response she gave him a wan smile. Already the knee was returning to normal. Perhaps it was not the knee that was weak; the effect of teleportation on her equilibrium might well account for it. That was something she would have to check out at the base in Brazil—after-effects on the cochlea, and the sense of balance. Travel with Matt happened too quickly. Normally one experienced a journey, and was aware of the passing of time and distance. There was scenery, and—depending on the airlines—free peanuts or drinks. On occasion there was luggage to manage.

That last thought reminded her that recently Matt had purchased various items on his credit card and that as yet she had not seen them with him. She wondered what they were, and how they might be concerned with his plans, whatever they were.

"One more problem to solve," she said, her eyes now on the Cessna.

Matt made a face. "I figured as much. How to avoid being droned after we take off." He sighed, and turned away, muttering to himself. "The more I try to avoid all this, the further I'm dragged into it."

"I'm sorry, Matt."

"Sure you are."

Breath left her. "*Alors*, I am not sorry to be dragging you into this," she snapped. "That is my *job*. It is what I *do*. I am only sorry that you feel you are being dragged into this."

"That's way too meta for me." He dragged a hand through his hair. Already sweat had gathered there. He wiped it on his jeans, and looked at Jacques. "Do you have a view of your landing approach in Brazil?" he asked.

"Why would you need that?" asked Kerise, puzzled.

He heaved an impatient sigh. "Because without an image of the actual landing strip there, I cannot get the plane to it," he explained, his tone adding that he shouldn't have to. "So we're going to have to take off, and get in the air, and that's when I'll do the transfer. I'd like to emerge us onto his usual flight path, a couple miles or so from the landing strip, so that he can take you down. Ideally what I'd like to have is one of those terrain recordings like they have on cruise missiles to follow to their target." He turned to Jacques. "Well?"

"You," said Kerise.

Matt shook his head at her, confused.

"You said Jacques would take 'you' down. Meaning us, not you."

"After we're over Brazil, I won't be aboard."

"Matt—"

"No! No more. No more, Kerise."

"Let him go," Analou said softly.

Matt continued to gaze expectantly at Jacques. Finally the pilot gave a little nod. "I have a recording that is something like what you seek," he said.

⁂

Lost, Hartland moaned silently. The opportunity

missed. It was falling apart. It had fallen apart. Two powerful paranormals were on the loose and aware that they were being hunted. A rogue intelligence agent who might have been able to tell them more about the current wave of terrorist attacks had been spotted, and had vanished before he could be relocated. Worst of all, she was stuck here in French Lick, Indiana, because Echelon did not have enough political voice at the moment to take her back to Washington.

She returned to her café table. The latte was still there, although some had spilled when she had shot to her feet. She sat down and tested it. It was tepid. Even the afternoon sun had failed to keep it hot enough. Her cracked Palmetto still functioned after a fashion, but issued so much static around voices at the other end of the link that it was useless to try to communicate. Doubtless a big box existed somewhere in this miserable little city. Possibly the GPS in the rental car could help her. At the moment, she felt no urge to move.

Again she sipped her latte, and frowned into the mug. Was that a dead fly? The realization nauseated her. She set the mug aside. Hot air seemed to come from nowhere to envelop her. A shadow fell on her; she looked up. The face looked familiar—thin, angular, with a jutting jaw and a straight nose that had been broken at least once. Eyes of blue ice. Shock of dark brown hair that did not take kindly to grooming. He had shed his suit coat somewhere, but still looked overly warm in a white dress shirt with a dull red necktie, and charcoal gray trousers. She was unable to see his shoes, but undoubtedly they were soft-soled, else she might have detected his approach before his shadow arrived.

The familiarity reduced her defenses. A wave of her hand invited the man to sit down. He did so. He had a benevolent, tolerant smile, as if he knew she was searching her memory, without success, for his identity. He did not let her suffer long.

"Francis Church," he said. He did not offer to shake hands.

Hartland thought about that, matched the name to a memory, and gave a little start. "Frank. Of course." She eyed him, trying to reconcile the present with the past. "What's it been, ten years?"

"Twelve."

"And still with The Company."

Church shook his head. "Seven years ago, I took a lateral transfer to R&D, DCI. Same grade at the time, GS-17. It's GS-19 now."

The phrasing almost brought a wrinkle to her brow. In the language they both spoke, "took" meant that he had sought the transfer, as opposed to receiving it involuntarily. It meant he had a motive for doing so.

Hartland issued a perfunctory, "Congratulations." It was strange that they should meet here, but she was unable to put her finger on what, exactly, was wrong. Still, it seemed safe to ask, "But what are you doing here?"

"Cutting to the chase, as usual, I see." He drew a folded sheet of fine stationery from his shirt pocket and passed it across the table to her.

For a mad moment she thought she was being handed a summons to appear in court. The frown made her forehead ache as she opened it and read it. She read it a second time before she tried to speak. Her throat was dry; she lubricated it with cold coffee, the fly forgotten.

"You're taking over?" she croaked. Her tone said, "You can't *do* that to me."

Church shrugged. "It's the DCI's call to make," he reminded her.

"You-you want to weaponize them."

"Don't you?"

"But—"

Church leaned forward, his eyes boring into hers. "Where are they, Geneva?"

"I certainly don't know. I need to—"

"You need to bring me up to speed."

Hartland sputtered. The sound astonished her. She did not know she could make it. "Right here?" she said, with a glance around her. Nobody else was anywhere near earshot.

"Right here. Right now."

022

Columbus, Ohio

In Columbus, Matt took a motel room under an assumed name, and paid for it with cash. It was not much more than a roof over his head, which was all he needed at the moment. Parting with Kerise had proved more emotional than he had expected. He stretched out on the bed, laced his fingers under his head, and tried to shut his mind to the memory.

It broke through his defenses.

He had expected her to cry, and was mentally prepared for the pitiful artifice of tears. What he had not expected was the discovery that the tears were sincere, and welled from deep within her. Her hand on his arm. Her proximity, as if she wanted to hold onto him and not let go. The gleam of her wet, silver eyes. The heat he felt...had someone opened the hatch when the airplane emerged near the equator?

He had transferred, before anything else could happen. Or had he fled? Either was, the result was the same. Wasn't it?

When he was with the girl on the beach at La Jolla, he had called out Kerise's name. Why?

The mouth in his mind grated the words out: I can't be a part of this.

Jesse...

He shed a tear, and another. I miss you, bro.

He made a fist. Knuckles whitened. Nails threatened to draw blood.

Abruptly he sat up. From a pocket of his jeans he withdrew and unfolded a map he had downloaded from Google. Today was Tuesday...he checked the time app on his Palmetto. Yes, it was after midnight. The three-day window opened today. He was over-wrought. Meditation... but he needed something else, too. What time would it be, there? Just after nine?

He summoned the image, and transferred.

Once again Matt found himself on the beach at the La Jolla Cove. He hadn't thought ahead. Others were about when he emerged before the girl with the anime face. He could feel them gaping at him, not quite certain what had just occurred. The late twilight dulled their disbelief; perhaps they had not witnessed what he had just done.

"Whoa!" she exclaimed.

He smiled. "Yeah."

Others around him backed away, shaking their heads. One or two stared at the can in their hands, as if it were the fault of the beer. Out of the corner of his eye Matt spotted a child of about eight or nine, pointing to him. His mother swatted the arm down: don't point.

The girl said, "You, too."

The sun had just set. Already the brightest stars had winked in. They reminded him that, in theory, he could go anywhere he wanted. And do anything he wanted. Stars represented freedom. He had freely chosen to seek out this girl.

She gestured to the blanket she had just spread on the sand. They sat down. As before, it was not necessary to say anything, but to listen to the sounds of the ocean. The screes of seagulls punctuated the sentences of the waves. The arms of the cove enclosed him and her in parentheses. She had sat down just close enough for him to feel warmer. She was wearing denim cutoffs, ragged at the hem and torn over her right hip. Pale skin glowed through the tear. She was wearing a string top as black as her long loose hair. She smelled of salt and lilacs. He dug his fingers into the blanket, enclosing a glob of sand with the fabric, fighting with himself. He was uncertain what he wanted, or why he had come. For her, yes, but no, not for her.

After the shock of his arrival, she acted as if emerging from thin air were the most natural thing in the world. Something everyone did.

Waves continued their sudden appearance, marching up the steep incline of the cove toward the shore to die. But each one died a little further away; the tide was ebbing.

Ebb Tide, thought Matt. That was a song on the Oldies station. He did not recall the melody. He relaxed on the blanket. His thoughts were his own. The girl beside him wanted nothing from him, nor was she involved in a project that required his involvement. She was simply there. If he wanted to share what he was thinking, he could do so. She would not broach her words uninvited. The silence of the waves and the stars clung to them.

I wonder what her name is.

Do I really want to know?

After tonight, I'll never see her again.

Again he clutched the blanket tightly. He should have been dealing with Jesse's killer. Why had he come here?

He knew the answer to that. Because I need to be with someone tonight, and there's too much turmoil around Kerise.

It wasn't, he decided, much of an excuse.

"Kerise," he whispered, involuntarily.

"It's Lilac," she said softly.

He gave a light laugh. "That explains the scent."

But words died with the waves, and with the meteor that raced across the night sky.

Matt lost all awareness of the passing of time. Minutes marched like waves into an hour, and more than. The few beach fires were allowed to die down. Sand and sea water was thrown over them. People began to leave. A few stragglers remained, all at the other end of the cove, the last remnants of a college group. He could just make out a few voices over the rush and hiss of the waves. They were not sounds that could concern him.

"Are you cold?" he asked her.

In response, she scooted a little closer to him. "Not so much, now."

"Lilac—"

"Like the song says, love the one you're with."

"Stephen Stills. I remember some of the lyrics. Including those."

She sighed. "Our longest conversation."

"Something for your diary."

"I keep it here," she said, tapping the side of her head. "I can see what I want to see, but nobody else can, unless

I let them."

"I'm Matt," he blurted, unable to stop himself.

"Oh."

He gave her a sidelong glance. "Is that bad?"

"No. I thought it was Jesse."

Breath left him as if his chest had just been flattened. He twisted on the blanket to stare at her. Dark eyes glowed back at him. His mouth finally worked. "How— Where did—"

"Afterwards," she answered easily. "I liked watching you sleep. I counted your REMs. It was the only name you spoke. My only point of reference."

"For your diary."

"Why, yes."

Matt tried to gather himself. He wanted to do his breathing exercises, to calm him for meditation. Gradually it sank in that he could do them; the girl would not interfere, nor would she leave him. He closed his eyes, took three deep breaths through his nose and released them through his mouth, and proceeded to clear his mind of all thought and all sensation. The waves crashed? He noted the sounds and set them aside. A gull cried? He filed that over there. The girl touched his hand? Put it aside. He saw nothing.

He saw Kerise.

Kerise morphed into Lilac.

Love the one you're with.

Along his perimeter, her voice came lower, and husky now. "You're troubled."

Blinking, he came out of the meditation. "I guess it shows."

"I'm sorry," she said. "I wouldn't have spoken. But your breathing quickened, so I knew you were on the verge of coming back to me."

"How long—

"I don't know," she answered. "Possibly an hour, more."

"Jesse was my kid brother."

"Is, not was."

He shook his head. "He's dead."

"Not as long as you remember him."

"You're so meta."

"But you know it's true."

"Yes…"

It occurred to him that he'd made the same rejoinder to both women. Yet they were hardly the same, or even similar. Lilac was the Sea of Tranquility. Kerise was the edge of a precipice.

"What happened?" Lilac asked.

Matt had no desire to answer, yet he did not want to deny Lilac. The conflict surprised him. Where had it come from? Why was it so difficult for him to pass on with a simple, "I'd rather not say," and let it go at that?

The waves lulled him. Slowly he gave in.

"We were in the Army together," he said, offering her only the barest outline. "We were sent to Syria, to fight a war we should never have been involved it. We were not defending the country—had we been, dying would have been easier. Disappointing, but easier."

The thoughts and memories flowed more quickly now, and he sorted through them for the most clear and concise.

"No one in the military has died defending the country since 1945," he went on, now with controlled fury. "They've died for someone's foreign policy. For someone's big-power game."

"Like World War I," inserted Lilac.

He nodded. "That's an excellent example. At one point, the Allies sent fresh British troops across no-man's-land, between the trenches, in the hopes that the Germans would run out of bullets. When the Americans arrived, the Allies wanted to do the same thing with them. General Pershing told them to stuff it."

"But what about Nine Eleven?"

"We were attacked, that's true," he replied. "But Saudi Arabia provided the funding and most of the personnel. Pakistan provided support as well as safe refuge for the masterminds. But the administration regarded those two countries as our friends. Afghanistan had provided a training ground for al-Qaeda, although it had no part in or knowledge of the attacks on the United States. So we chose to attack them. We had a subtle game in mind: if we could bring Afghanistan to its knees, it would demonstrate our superiority to the Russians, who fought there for a decade with nothing to show for it but a waste of men and money and the downfall of Communism. So now we've been dying there for onto three decades now, and we just signed our troops on for another five years. It's the Belgian trenches all over again."

Matt paused to drag a hand through his hair and to recompose after delivering himself of his rant. In the silence, he feared he had come off as a conspiracy theorist. But Lilac seemed not to notice. Maybe she grasped that he needed to get this out.

Calmer, he went on, "The attack on the training area of Afghanistan was justified, and we obliterated it. But the masterminds had anticipated our response—how could they not?—and had already flown the coop. So we got this really neat idea. We decided to make them, and Iraq, and the whole Middle East into democracies, just like us. Never mind that constitutional democracy and the Quran are incompatible. The whole world has got to be just like us—"

Lilac held up a hand. "Wait," she said softly. "How are they incompatible?"

"Okay, in a constitutional democracy, in theory if not always in practice, the constitution is the highest authority in the land. It tells the government what it can and cannot do, it establishes protections for basic rights, and it even provides a mechanism for changing it. But in Muslim countries, the highest authority is the Quran, which is The Word of God. How do you change The Word of God?"

"Oh."

"Which is why women have to dress just so, and go out of the house accompanied by a male relative, and are restricted from driving," he said. "Which is why Muslims are directed to kill infidels. True, there are lulls, when killing and violence are regarded as imprudent. The period between the World Wars is a good example of this; Muslims had very little military might, very little power to effect wars with the infidels. Now they have weapons and ammo and military might—thanks to us, in large part because either we gave them that, or because they captured it from our troops there."

"And... Jesse?"

"Our misguided policies got him killed. He might as well have been murdered by— Well, anyway, there you are. I'm sorry to talk your ears off."

She pressed her lips against his shoulder. "You needed it. And..."

"And?"

"I have some other things you can talk off," she said. "But I'd rather do that in the camper. People might whisper and point."

023

French Lick, Indiana

After inspecting her hotel room with a critical eye and finding nothing to complain about—a disappointment, that—Geneva Hartland settled into the stuffed chair by the window and tried not to think about the developments of the past day. In one fell swoop her career and status had come to an end—a swoop conducted under the auspices of the Deputy Chief of Staff for Intelligence, GS-19 Frank Church presiding. In taking over Echelon and terminating her leadership of it, he had spoken with the forthrightness of a screwdriver applying the last twist to a wood screw, seating it fully into the plank. That it had been done to her—a reversal of fortunes—grated, the more so because she was helpless to oppose it.

Even more grating was the designation of Oliver West as her replacement. In retrospect, she realized she should have seen this coming. For years her Chief of Security had concealed a conniving, nefarious mind under a façade of meek deference. Yet he knew relatively little about the Echelon program itself...didn't he? Well, his long game had reached fruition; now the end game began. She needed now to conceptualize her involvement in it.

Most significant of Church' announcement—and here she wondered whether he was even aware of it—was his seemingly inadvertent revelation that Echelon testing had turned up others, not from military sources but from schools and universities. What was the word he used to describe the quantity? A few? She thought back. Yes, there were a few more out there, waiting to be snapped up. And here she was, without any position in the snapping organization.

She got up and stepped to a counter, where a small bucket of ice waited. A Chivas mini over a rock was just what she wanted at the moment. Fortified, she returned to the stuffed chair and lost herself in the view through the window. It had been a day to question what was going on, not just with Echelon and DCI, but with the country. The U.S. was starting to fall apart, attacked from without and within, not only by an implacable enemy, but by its own citizens who presumed to know what was best for everyone. Social and news media and schools could do only so much to bring about social conformity. Human beings were by nature contrary and rebellious. Mind control could change all that. And that was the projected function of the Paranormals.

Except how did one control the Paranormals?

It was a question that to date had not found a solution. Control drugs dampened the paranormal ability. In theory, most paranormals could easily flee from physical coercion. That left persuasion: they had to come to understand that what they were being asked to do was right. So far, the argument had fallen flat.

Hartland downed the remainder of her drink and went to fix another one.

I should have just brought a fifth, she thought.

⚬⚬⚬

Munich, Germany

Langford opted to walk the streets. Having been given the flash drive with the secret data made him the better target—a reasonable point Sylvie had made. She would have preferred to, as she said, "do the streetwalking," and she did not understand why Langford thought that was funny. He decided not to explain it to her; she was, after all, armed.

Over the weekend they had become lovers. A little thought nagged at Langford regarding their newfound relationship, that for Sylvie the need was more physiological than emotional, the opposite for him. For them, sex was *pro tempore* and *ad hoc*, and probably *nolo contendere* as well. It was not built to last, but to be enjoyed while it lasted. Langford felt guilty.

Not that he was fastidious or squeamish. He'd had relationships before that had lasted for weeks, or a couple of weekends, even a couple of hours. He'd had few with relative strangers; none, really.

Langford stood on the balcony in the morning sun, contemplating all this. That, too, formed part of his guilt. He knew that it should not be thought about, merely accepted; it had been so before. What made this different?

The destination for that train of thought faded with her touch on his bare arm. "Is it that you are married?" she inquired.

He had to laugh. "Just now you think to ask me?" He patted her hand. "The answer is no. Why?"

"Because you are acting the guilt," she replied. "It is bad for your aura."

"Maybe we should let my aura walk the streets."

She laughed, a sound that three days ago he would have been astonished to hear her emit. Her cheek rested against his shoulder for a moment. "I will be watching you," she promised.

"In disguise."

"*Biensûr.* Even you will not recognize me. This is why you must not see me put on the disguise."

On a fingertip she held out a piece of cream-colored plastic the size and shape of an aspirin. On one side, the adhesive gleamed, ready for application. He ducked his head, and she pressed the pill under his left earlobe, where it would be concealed from the greatest view.

"How does it look?" he asked.

She gave it a full inspection, from up close, and from five paces away. "The person who would recognize it as artificial, would frighten me. *Un moment.*" She stepped into the closet and pulled the door shut.

Presently he heard her voice: "*Tu m'écoutes?*"

"*Oui. Et tu?*"

"*Cinq pour cinq.*" She emerged from the closet. "I have the volume correct on the first attempt," she announced. "*Eh bien. Allons-y.*"

Langford's heard skipped. Now it begins, he thought.

⁂

La Jolla Cove, California

Sunlight through the rear window of the camper awoke Matt. At some point after the love, the single blanket they had slept under had become bunched along the left side of the inflatable mattress. In the dark, they had found each other with their hands and bodies. Now, in the daylight, he had a different view of her. It did not arouse him. Instead, he was able to see her as a vision, a dream. She was not beautiful, as men regarded that quality. In fact, aside from the anime face, her body was unremarkable in its appearance. Except that he had mapped it with his fingertips, and enjoyed the cartography.

"Romantic," she murmured, and sat up.

"About ten minutes," he said, in answer to her unspoken question.

She sighed. "Nature calls."

"After you."

Matt dressed reluctantly. There had been moments around midnight when doubts had crept in. The only decision he was happy with, was to come back to see Lilac. He'd wondered, in the dark, how he would feel when he actually moved to avenge Jesse. Not planned it, not envisioned it, not prepared for it—but went to do it. Because of all the decisions he had to make, this one, once acted upon, was irrevocable.

"I have to go," he said.

"I know."

"Lilac—"

She hushed him with a finger across his lips. "I am not sorry that I am not Kerise for you," she told him. "I am happy to be Lilac for you. I wish that you would have both of us." She gave him a little shove. "Go now. Do whatever it is that you must do, that takes you away from the women who hold your heart. But come back to us both."

His brow rumpled with the notion. She gave him no time to consider it.

"Go," she urged. "Now."

024

Northwest Brazil

Kerise was sitting on her bed, pondering a moment when she had sat there with Matt. Her heart ached. Previously she had thought that a figure of speech, but no—it actually ached. She rubbed the spot; it failed to alleviate the pain. She fought against her mood with a flickering smile, but lost. Eyes moist now, she rubbed them with the palms of her hands. This only caused tears to flow.

She had thought she knew all that she needed to know about Matthew Porter, based on the extensive document-ation Indigo had accumulated over the past three years. That alone was enough to make her fall in love with him. She wanted him in the project because of the abilities he offered, yes, but the bottom line was that she wanted him, period. And now he was gone. The project had not been enough to dissuade him from his self-appointed task, whatever it was. To use her body as an incentive might have been something she was prepared to do, if necessary, with someone else of his abilities, but not with him. She would never forgive herself for the insincerity, and probably neither would he.

Not that it had been easy to restrain her libido.

She drew a shuddering breath, held it, and let it out in a series of puffs. It eased nothing.

At the gentle knock at her door, she looked up to see Anastasia Louise Somerville standing in the doorway. At her diffident, "May I come in?" Kerise made a feeble gesture. Analou sat down at the foot of the bed, clasped her hands together, and held them between her knees as she hunched forward. She did not look at Kerise. She kept her voice low, and non-threatening.

"You," she said, "are a dark cloud of gloom."

Kerise, who had been anticipating some form of sympathy, barked a mirthless laugh.

"That's how I 'see' you," sniffed Analou.

"Empaths," Kerise muttered.

"I have other talents."

A twinge of guilt swatted Kerise. Of course the woman would have other talents. Blinded by her focus on Matt, she hadn't kept herself open to other possibilities.

"For instance?" she said.

Analou nibbled her lip, as if hesitating to divulge some personal information that no one else knew. "I can act on objects at a distance," she said slowly, finding her way. "I'm sure you know this."

"You lifted that pickup truck."

She acknowledged this with a tight nod. "And a few other things." She paused, and turned to gaze at Kerise for long seconds. "I haven't tried—I haven't even thought about it—but I might be able to transport us. A few minutes ago, when I was in the bathroom, I managed to move a roll of tissue to the utility closet. What I did not do, or try to do, was move myself with it."

"Is this something you want to try?" asked Kerise.

"I-I don't know. I'm not sure. It could be dangerous."

"As long as we don't wind up in Katmandu."

Analou chuckled. She was about to comment when Teague showed up in the doorway. His expression was grimmer than Kerise had ever seen it before. He stood straight there, weight evenly distributed on both legs, hands jammed with finality into his front pockets. He seemed to be staring through her at something in his imagination. Kerise and Analou kept silent.

Finally he said, "Something has happened. I don't know what. They've shut down the entire country. Nobody in or out. No flights, no shipments, no trucks and buses, nothing. Some National Guards have been called out, but to do what, nobody is saying."

"The attacks?" asked Analou.

He shook his head as if he had already considered this, and found it wanting. "Something more grave than that. I don't know...a domestic nuclear threat, maybe. I have a contact."

"Rother," said Kerise.

Teague nodded. "He's the one who told me. But he had close commo right away, and I do mean instantly. Even so, they may ask him questions...unkindly. I told your dad as well." His face twisted in a rictus of annoyance. "If this sets us back..."

"As you say, we don't know what happened," said Kerise. "Let's give it a couple of days and see what shakes out."

"That's just about what your dad told me."

⁕

La Jolla Cove, California

Blue lights flashing, the police car passed slowly along the parking area that overlooked the cove. At each vehicle it paused, as if the driver were making a list of license plate numbers. Twice they had actually halted behind Lilac's camper. The second time, a helicopter had passed overhead, but Lilac managed to avoid the searchlight by submerging herself. She was just taking a twilight dip, along with several other folks.

In the water, she trembled. The temperature was warm enough—the cove was always warm—but the presence of the police and the helicopter set her teeth on edge. She hadn't done anything in particular to warrant their interest, but she had no doubt they were looking for her. She'd locked the camper, but that wouldn't stop them.

Could it be Matt? Did they *know* about him, and that he had been seen with her? She didn't see how that could be. But if they were not looking for her in connection with him, then—

Shit, she thought. *Shit shit shit.* They *know.* They're here for *me.*

⁕

Columbus, Ohio

Matt's heart raced as he stood shivering inside the abandoned gas station. It had rained all day, and a north wind had dropped the temperature to unseasonable lows. So focused had he been, he hadn't thought to wear a jacket, or at least a windbreaker. Jesse would have laughed at him.

So far, so good. He had obtained a schematic and photographs of the target building. He had wound up in the closet. He hadn't had long to wait. The couple came into the bedroom, laughing the way married people did now and then. He might have emerged then, but he would have had to take her as well. He'd waited for almost three years. He could wait a few more minutes.

Presently he'd heard the sounds of disrobing. Footsteps approached the closet where he was hiding behind the other clothes on the hangers. The door opened. A suit coat was thrust in his direction. He grabbed the arm and yanked the man into the closet, and pressed a chloroformed handkerchief to his nose before he could cry out. In the next moment, they were gone.

Simple.

Complicated.

Inside the station his chest continued to shudder with each shallow breath he drew. He made fists to calm himself; his heart and lungs ignored him. He was caught between "I did it!" and "What have I done?"

Matt had not been seen in the room. Possibly the man's wife had caught a glimpse of shadow. She could testify that there was just the one abductor, nothing more damning than that. Gradually the sense of accomplishment began to overwhelm the anxiety and alarm of his actions. Jesse was being avenged.

His heart rate slowed, and his respiration became deeper. Normalized, he slumped against a wall. Strength returned to his buckling knees. Still, he needed to rest—to gird himself for the confrontation. The image of his room in the nearby motel coalesced into focus.

He found himself there.

⁓

French Lick, Indiana

Frank Church pressed his earbud against the side of his head as he poked his way through the debris. He had gained entry into the room previously occupied by Matthew Porter, there to seek clues as to Porter's current whereabouts. It had already become obvious to him that he needed to return to headquarters in Maryland and regroup. Getting himself to Maryland was the problem.

"What about an F-35?" he asked Oliver West, who was still at Echelon in Maryland.

"Nothing flies, Frank. I'm sorry. You'll have to wait this out."

"What about our other candidates? Can we get to them?"

"We're working on that now," West replied. "Unfortunately, we've had to ground everything, except the drones. We're tracking one candidate, even as we speak. But if she poofs out, we've lost her... temporarily, at least."

"And the P—"

"*Don't* say it!" yelled West.

"Right. But what about him?"

"Nothing yet. His wife is no help. She saw nothing."

"It's gotta be... you know who."

A mild static filled a brief hesitation. "I might have a plan there, to bring him out into the open. Our overseas assets are still active, and have transportation. Check back in the morning, Frank."

"Understood," said Church, to a dead phone.

La Jolla Cove, California

Despite the temperature already in the high seventies, the ocean air chilled Lilac. With the police and other officials searching for her, she had taken refuge in one of the caves in the shoreline rocks. The high tide had sealed it off, further protecting her. From her position she was able to see the camper, still parked at the top of the ridge overlooking the cove. Although no one was in the area at the moment, and no official vehicles were visible, she did not doubt that they were nearby, keeping watch. She assumed the camper had been searched, but they would have found nothing useful. Clothes, books, drawing pads, a set of pencils, charcoal sticks, plus the usual accouterments of a camper. She was almost but not quite a non-person, and there was nothing aboard to connect her to the so-called grid except registration and insurance.

The test she had taken in her junior year in high school, and another in her sophomore year at San Diego State, had to have turned them to her. Belatedly she had realized the tests had nothing to do with scholarship or learning ability, but at the time she could think of no other reason for them. After graduation, when she noticed that every time she used her plastic, the process seemed to take a little longer than was customary, and the usual excuses were wearing thin, she added two and two and came up with an imaginary number. Had some academic institution been monitoring her—Duke University was noted for paranormal studies—she might have accommodated the research. But the sort of passive surveillance in operation against her could only be performed by the government. She wanted no part of it.

Now they had found her. They knew she was in the vicinity. They assumed she would return at some point for her vehicle, her things. They were waiting.

Shivering, hugging herself, Lilac mulled over her choices. They were three. Disappear, and abandon the camper. Transport herself into the camper and drive away. Transport herself into the camper and disappear with it. Option two meant they would probably pursue her, most likely with the addition of drones. Options two and three entailed the risk that they had placed at least one tracer inside or on the camper. Option one meant abandoning her work—just some drawings and sketches, but dammit they were *hers*.

She looked down at herself. There weren't that many places in public she could go while wearing a wet royal blue string bikini.

And she could always steal some money and buy another camper...

Columbus, Ohio

Drowsy in the sunlight through the front window of the motel room, Matt dressed quickly, and sat down on the bed to gather himself. Today was the day. Jesse would be avenged. But.

But now that the moment was upon him, he was beginning to have misgivings. For one thing, no matter what he did to his captive, nothing would change. The wars from which the President had promised to withdraw U.S. forces were continuing unabated. They had cost Jesse his life. The broken promise had killed him just as surely as the bullets from the Syrian sniper had done. But Matt was wondering now whether revenge would be enough. Because nothing would change. Jesse wasn't coming back.

What is it that I want? he asked himself, sitting now at the edge of the bed. He had no answer other than the immediate, the obvious. After that...after that, various black agencies in the Federal government, especially Echelon, would figure out what had happened, and therefore who had done it, and he would be hounded relentlessly for the rest of his life. As they were already hounding Analou.

First things first. He stood up, envisioned his destination, and vanished from the room.

025

Munich, Germany

Langford wiped his forehead and hoped that sweat would not dissolve the adhesive that held his tracer in place. He dared not reveal its existence and location by putting a finger behind his ear to check. Waiting for the tram had caused him more anxiety than just walking around downtown Munich. This was the checkpoint. If he were being followed, his pursuers would have to identify themselves by boarding the tram as well. Not everyone who boarded the tram would be following him, but at least the possibilities would be narrowed down.

Assuming, of course, that he was in fact being followed.

Although he had been instructed not to, Langford looked around. The tram was half-full, and the smell of a gym room made him want to take short shallow breaths. He was familiar with the tightness of riding the tram, and knew well why there was often an accompanying aroma of rose water. He did not make eye contact with anyone, nor did he try to seek out Sylvie, who was somewhere aboard. He was, however, able to eliminate the two women in their thirties who were wearing nylons over unshaved legs. Both were bulkier than the French operative, and there was no possible way those were her slim ankles and calves in disguise.

The tram rounded a corner, horn blaring at a vehicle that had momentarily overridden the track in the middle of the street. Legally trams had the right-of-way, and very few vehicles had the temerity to challenge it. Suddenly suspicious, Langford rescanned the occupants of the tram, to see whether someone had jumped aboard as the tram had slowed. There was no one new. He was about to dismiss his concerns when someone jabbed him in the ribs from behind.

Langford spun around, eyes wide in alarm. Confronting him was an elderly woman who was prodding him with her umbrella. From her gestures and the few words he understood, she wanted to sit down, and he was blocking her path to the empty seat. Chagrined, he moved aside and let her pass.

The tram stopped, and two passengers disembarked. As far as Langford could tell, neither of them had gotten on with him. A mild paranoia began to set in: the two might be misdirection, intended to make him relax his guard.

One more stop, then. He found he could stand no more. The tram was approaching Goetheplatz and a small crowd out for lunch. He breathed slowly, deliberately, to recompose himself. Getting off at the square would blend him with the crowd and make it almost impossible for Sylvie to protect him. He decided to stay on for one more stop.

The tram coasted to a stop, iron wheels shrieking on iron rails. He did not move. Perhaps half a dozen passengers disembarked; he thought a couple of them had gotten on with him. The tram waited; it was a minute or so ahead of schedule, and that would not do.

Another jab in the ribs. As he turned to look, a man in a fedora leaned closer and whispered, "Not a sound. Act natural. We're getting off."

Langford heard the sound of a hard impact, followed immediately by a high-pitched moan. An umbrella withdrew from between the man's legs as he collapsed into Langford's arms.

The old woman got to her feet, more spry now. "He is drunk," Sylvie instructed him. "Let us get him off the tram."

⚓

Columbus, Ohio

The man blinked against the utter darkness and failed to promote so much as a spark. Metal chilled his back, and clung to his wrists and ankles. Realization struck him like a mallet: he was secured to a metal wall. And he was naked. His groin tightened involuntarily; at least that was still functioning. But the basic questions of information gathering met with silence. Who what where? When why? How huh?

He had just hung up his suit jacket. One arm in the closet, the other hand beginning to work at his necktie. Chemical-laden cloth against his nose. Chloroform? But who...*how*? *Impossible* that someone had snuck into his closet. Impossible that someone had *abducted* him...and so *easily*. One second, and bang! He was gone. Not a shot fired in his defense.

What's that smell? Very faint. Not chloroform...

A prime target, he could think of dozens of countries and organizations that would love to get their hands on him. Drugs...was this about drugs? The ubiquitous Mexican cartels? Or a preemptive act of war, cutting off the head? Omigod, did they get the Football, too?

What...what are they going to do to me?

Sudden fear stank like old sweat.

His bladder surrendered. Warm liquid trickled down his right leg. He heard droplets splash on the floor.

Floor, he thought. Where exactly am I?

"Hello?"

An echo answered him.

How long had it been? An hour? Seven?

Have they just left me here??

"Hello?" he shouted.

The resounding echo was deafening.

The smell. It's gasoline... Oh, no, they *wouldn't*. They wouldn't...

"Can you hear me? What...what do you want?"

Tears welled in his eyes. He swallowed hard.

He whimpered. "Answer me. Please, answer me."

"For the love of God answer me!"

"H-hello? Oh Godgodgod... Hello..."

Matt materialized in the dark. He'd left Jesse's killer without so much as a candle. Left him handcuffed and spread-eagled and naked against an inner wall of the empty gasoline reservoir at the abandoned station. Left him standing, for all the good it would do him. Maybe he'd gotten some sleep. Matt rather doubted it.

A voice made hoarse and gravelly from yelling, and still coherent. Matt hadn't bothered to gag him. There was no point in it; he had already assured himself that sound would not carry from the reservoir. He had also considered the possibility that the killer would be half-crazed by fear, being deprived of light and movement all night. Still, the man managed an obvious question.

"Who-who's there? Is s-someone there?"

Not the voice Matt had heard on television, making promises he had no intention of keeping. Not the confident voice of someone who knew he could not be defied or defeated. Not the steady voice of assurance. Not anymore.

Measured steps took Matt to the opposite wall. There he lit a votive candle and set it on the floor, and stepped back.

In the flickering light the man blinked several times. A jerk of his head cleared some strands of gray and brown hair that had fallen over his forehead and left eye. Matt had wondered what his first words would be upon seeing his captor, and learned that he had settled on the most likely. In the face of incredulity, bravado was often an initial attempt.

"Do you know who I am, young man?"

Candlelight showed that Jesse's killer had recovered some of his aplomb and arrogance. Matt shrugged. "Of course I know who you are, Mr. President," he said politely. "Carl Newcombe. You changed it from Karl with a K because it sounded Teutonic. Yes, I know exactly who you are."

That deflated the killer. A note of desperation set in, and he spoke quickly, as if he might not be allowed to finish speaking. "Who-who are you working for? The drug cartels? The Iranians? The Chinese? The Venezuelans? Who? Whatever they're paying you, I'll double it. Triple it."

"I'm working for Jesse Porter."

Newcombe's jaw dropped. He gulped like a hungry goldfish at fresh algae flakes. Finally he said, "W-who?"

Matt was ready for that question. "Despite your many promises to pull us out of the Middle East altogether upon your election, you sent him to Syria, where he was killed. I'm working for him. For his memory."

"You don't understand! There were much bigger issues involved—"

Matt waved him off. "You thought you were safe," he said, his anger growing. "You thought you could say anything and do anything. That's been your whole life, hasn't it? You avoided military service due to infected tonsils. You were pampered and protected from the type of lives most of us have to live. To you, Jesse was a warm body. He was head count. Just like all the other soldiers you sent over there after you promised not to. After you promised to pull us out, not put more of us in. His death and his blood are on your hands."

Matt paused, and added, "That's what this is all about, Mr. President."

"You-you *can't do* this to me!"

"I see your perception of reality is still as flawed as ever. Look around. Tell me what you see."

Newcombe did so. "It...it's a chamber of some kind. A metal chamber. No windows, no..." In a higher pitch, he said, "Wait... how did I get in here? How did *you*?"

"So the plan," Matt went on, "is to leave you here. I'll unlock your left hand. You can undo the others. I'll leave the candle burning. It will burn itself out in a few hours. You can do what Injun Joe did with his."

"W-who?"

"From *Tom Sawyer*? Never mind. You're much too egotistical to learn any new lessons, and I have no inclination to teach you. They'll always wonder what happened to you. You might even get your face on a postage stamp, in memorial." He drew a breath, calming himself. "For the murders of Jesse Porter and unknown, untold others, I sentence you to life in this prison. As there is no water in here, that shouldn't be much longer than three days. I'd guess insanity will settle in sooner than that." He rubbed his chin for a moment, then dug the handcuff keys from his pocket. "I suppose I could put a rat in here to make it interesting, but as it happens, I like rats. So long, Mr.

President."

"Wait. Please, just... wait."

He folded his arms across his chest, impatient. "What is it?"

"Where... am I? If I'm going to die here, I'd at least like to know where this is."

"Very well. You're in the methanol gas reservoir of a closed-down gas station in Columbus, Ohio. Your mausoleum, as it were."

"That's not possible."

"No more possible than sneaking into your bedroom at Camp David and bringing you here. Oh, and you don't have to worry about jet lag, as the trip only took a couple of seconds."

Take it easy, Matt told himself. Don't get giddy with success. No euphoria. This is not an accomplishment. You've kept a promise. The end result is not something to be proud of. Satisfied, perhaps.

He stepped forward to undo the left handcuff. A buffet of displaced air made him whirl around. The candle flickered and almost went out. In the dim light stood Lilac.

⚬⚬⚬

Northwest Brazil

Simon-Louis Renaud finally found a few moments in which to sit at his desk. Accustomed to the sight and feel of the fine teakwood, he'd had it brought by a circuitous route from France to the subterranean development in Brazil. Kerise was proficient at arranging such deceptions, and might have made an excellent smuggler or, earlier in history, a pirate. He lounged back in his office chair and laced his fingers behind his head, while he considered recent black and secure reports he had received through various sources and cut-outs.

The President of the United States of America was missing. He had been abducted from his bedroom at Camp David. As yet, no one had claimed responsibility for the deed, and no one had communicated a ransom demand. Having resolved to leave Earth, Renaud had scant interest in such events, except that in this instance the government response affected his operations. Nothing was going out of the country, and very little was getting in, none of it without a search of every cubic inch. Renaud had items on order.

He was not a tall or imposing man; his daughter was taller, and she had gotten her carrot hair from her mother, not from his brown-hair genes. At fifty-four he was in racquetball-shape, and ran two miles every other day, but even so, whenever he took to the sidewalk in Paris, from one building to another, no one paid him any mind. He preferred it that way. Only a handful of people knew him well.

One of whom was Kerise. His thoughts drifted to her. She was his Abu Bakr. Indigo was his conception, but Kerise was the true believer. She never did anything unless it was worth involving herself heart and soul. She was devoted to him, and in return he indulged her. Her plan to use paranormals in the Indigo Project seemed a waste of time to him, but she had done her homework and was adamant as to her course of action. Perhaps unfortunately, she had also fallen in love with one of the paranormals, even before she had actually met him. Renaud was beginning to wonder whether she had become sidetracked, whether her other duties were suffering. So far, the answer was no. But she was now stuck in Brazil, when he needed her in the U.S.

He had also learned that Echelon was under new management. The Office of the Deputy Chief of Staff for Intelligence had assumed command of Echelon operations. In doing so, information had been developed that might enable Kerise to achieve her objective. The question now was whether he should pass that information on to her. He'd asked her to his office, which meant he had less than five minutes now to decide.

The knock at his door came early. She always knocked, even though of all the people involved with the Project, she was the only one who would burst right in upon knocking, like a whirlwind, even before an invitation to enter was issued. It had become a game to them, over the past few years. He glanced up, and there she was. For the occasion she had chosen a pair of green slacks, a matching tube top, and an open, floral-print vest. Instead of her usual black boots, she was shod in a pair of brown loafers that did not go with the rest of the outfit at all. For a moment he considered whether the outfit was intended as some sort of statement, fashion or otherwise, and cast it aside. She wore what she felt like wearing. If others disapproved, that was on them.

She sprawled onto one of the two armchairs, one leg draped over an arm of it, her arms extended along the top of the back. The relaxed attitude was not reflected in her eyes. There he saw a cloud of concern.

Renaud opened the door in the right pedestal and withdrew a pair of Waterford lead crystal tumblers and a bottle of Chambord. Moments later they were both in armchairs, sipping, eyeing one another over the rims of the tumblers. She had nothing to say, but merely waited, a patient smile on her face and in her eyes; he had, after all, summoned her, and not the other way around.

He decided to present the news update direct and hard, without embellishment. Kerise was much like her mother, God rest her soul: frivolous, yes, but with a spine of iron when needed.

Renaud cleared his throat. "The U.S. has been closed down because the President has been abducted," he told her. "Nobody knows—"

Kerise sat bolt upright, slothing the drink on her slacks. "*Mon Dieu! C'est Matt! Mais non, non...*" Tears began to well in her silver eyes, and she wiped them away angrily. "Oh no..."

A worried frown darkened Renaud's face. "Kerise?"

She shook her head and clenched her fists and her teeth. "I am fine," she insisted fiercely. "Go on, please."

"If you're sure—"

"*Please*, Papa."

He sat back and crossed his legs. "Very well. Nobody knows where or why or by whom...although I suspect you do. The Vice President has been sworn in, as prescribed by law, but for now that fact is classified at the highest level. There has been no ransom demand."

"There won't be," said Kerise. "This was an act of revenge."

"I see," said Renaud, although he didn't, quite. He continued. "There is no telling how long this state of emergency will last. I believe it threatens to disturb our timetable. The news broadcasts you prepared and disseminated will also be affected, as we may not have departed before they are published."

"As always, your sources are excellent."

He acknowledge the praise with a curt nod. "For the price I am paying, they had better be. Now, then: we have developed information from Echelon. First, it is now run by DCI."

"They want to weaponize the paranormals," she said.

"If that's possible. The point is that three more have turned up." He ticked the names off on his fingers. "Pedro Villegas in San Juan, P.R. Nuala Lowry in California. Elvin Gilbreath, who is already in custody and sedated. You have connections that can get you into Puerto Rico surreptitiously."

"No," said Kerise.

"Yes, you do. Joshua Berimbu—"

She shook her head. "That's not what I meant, Papa. It has to be—it's going to be—Matt."

"Kerise, I cannot allow you to jeopardize—"

She stood up and began to pace the room. "And I won't, Papa. I think I know why Matt did it, and I think I know, within the boundaries of a city, where he is. All I have to do is get Analou and myself there."

"And Teague."

"Not this time. He's becoming unstable. Do you recall telling me that when he starts to come unraveled, he'll mix his consonants when he swears? Well, he's doing it. Sucking fop stign. Spucking leed fimit. Whatever you're paying him, he's growing more and more anxious to get it."

"But can you get into the U.S.?"

She sighed. "Maybe." She turned to go. "I'll let you know."

"Kerise," he said, and she turned around. "Be careful."

"*Biensûr*, Papa."

⁂

The Pentagon

After Lieutenant Colonel Albert Rother marched into the office of General Preston R. Welles, the Army Chief of Staff, and saluted as he reported in, he was not invited to one of the armchairs that circled in front of Welles' desk. Instead, not having been told to stand at ease, he remained at rigid attention. Rother had expected this treatment, and was prepared to spend hours, if necessary, in that position. With his eyes straight ahead, he was barely able to detect Welles in his peripheral vision, but he knew what he would see. In uniform Welles almost listed to his left due to the weight of his medals and honors. What hair remained to him was shorn to within a couple millimeters of his scalp. He had the hard face of a drillmaster, and the hard look of a detective intimidating a murder suspect.

Welles hefted a newspaper, and swatted it down on his desk as if to smite a fly. His voice was an iron bar banged against concrete. "Have you seen the morning's papers, Rother?"

"No, sir."

Welles opened the paper. "This one is the *Post*. The headline says, 'Pentagon Warned in Advance of Imminent Attack.' You're identified as the source for this article."

"Yes, sir."

He slapped the paper down again. "Right now, for a start, you're looking at unauthorized disclosure of classified information, and insubordination. I have no doubt that General Sutcliffe is preparing other charges arising from your actions. Sending your report to this office was proper under the circumstances. Sending it to the *Post* was a betrayal of the service and your oath. Your career isn't on the line here, Rother. It's *over*."

He slammed a fist down on his desk. Rother's eyes did not waver. "*Damn* it, man! Twenty-seven thousand people are dead, and the country is blaming *us*, not the Muslims, because of articles like this. They're saying we should have acted. We could have done more to save lives. Yet the attacks began in this time zone just a few seconds after you informed Sutcliffe. We did all that we could, and more." He paused. "Haven't you anything to say? Oh, stand at ease, for Christ's sake!"

Now Rother was free to look at him. He noted the red face, the sheen of sweat on the forehead, the tic at the corner of the left eye. "Sir," he said, and found his thoughts jumbled. What was there to say? "Sir, the information was not classified when I sent it to the Post and others. As regards insubordination, General Sutcliffe wanted to make sure his report and mine jibed. That's code for making my report match his. I don't believe much could have been done in the Eastern Time Zone, because of the late hour, and I did mention that in my report. What I was attacking, what I meant to attack, was the utter incredulity with which the information was received. Precious seconds were wasted. They might not have made much difference. General Sutcliffe's first action was not to call HomeSec, but to have his secretary call his wife and..."

"Yes, and his mistress," growled Welles. "I'm well aware of General Sutcliffe's dalliance, as is now the entire country. It's that fact, as much as anything else, that has sealed your fate, Colonel." He sat back. "Very well. Give a man enough rope... Colonel, you are confined to your quarters at the BOQ pending the results of our investigation. You are to speak of these events to no one. You are not to speak to a member of the press under any circumstances whatsoever. You will keep your phone with you at all times. When someone wants to see you, you will be summoned by phone." He fingered the newspaper again, and shook his head. "This was not necessary, Colonel," he went on. "I wonder why you did it. To cover your ass vis-à-vis General Sutcliffe's report? That doesn't seem likely. And you don't fit the profile of someone who seeks the limelight. Very well. Have you any questions?"

"No, sir."

"Dismissed."

Rother came to attention, saluted, and did a smart about-face before marching out of the office, intent on the parking lot and his Subaru. He had no qualms about what he had done. It would be nice to put in for retirement—he had over twenty years in service—and he meant to call

Admin to start the process, even though he doubted that retirement would be permitted. He had some funds put away, and some investments, and he made a mental note to cash them out as soon as possible. In the meantime...

He pulled out his Palmetto and found the coded number for Teague. He'd give him a call this evening. He tocked another set of numbers, and the deep blue car before him started right up.

026

Munich, Germany

It was no easy task for Langford and Sylvie to tumble the man into her car, but they managed it without attracting much attention. Sylvie smiled ingratiatingly at a couple of passers-by, murmuring something about her brother having too much to drink, and they nodded understandingly and moved on. Once the man was seated in back, Sylvie bound his wrists with a zip strip, and slid in beside him while Langford drove.

The man slowly regained his senses. From time to time Langford glanced at him in the rearview mirror, but Sylvie had him under control. Langford heard his questions, spoken first in German, then in English, but left the conversation to Sylvie. This was, after all, her business.

Langford took the autobahn south toward Bad Tölz, and then the exit that led out into farmland. Here the roads were as Sylvie had described them to him: two lanes of asphalt looping over rolling terrain, with pastures delineated by barbed wire and occupied by small herds of dairy cattle. A few of them at the fences stopped chewing their cuds as Langford drove by. Trees lined creeks, and gathered in sparse copses. Langford began to feel that what he and Sylvie were about to do would in some way violate the picturesque, jigsaw-puzzle quality of the countryside.

At last they reached a stone cottage on a small plot of land, almost hidden from the roadway by older trees and some unpruned vines. Langford pulled onto the gravel driveway and stopped in front on the turnaround. By this time the man in back had fallen silent, his questions unsatisfied. Before they got out, Sylvie said quietly, "I do not have to kill you. But you will not be my first."

Glowering, the man nodded. It was now clear to Langford that he was a professional, although his specialty had yet to be determined. He did not attempt to flee as they led him to the front door. Langford paused at the door, uncertain.

"No doors are locked around here," Sylvie told him.

He pushed the door open, and held it for her, closing it after she pushed the man inside.

Sparsely furnished, the main room featured two old armchairs, a table chair, and an end table. Langford had seen better quality at yard sales. The air was not as fetid as one might expect—just musty, with no spoiled food or anything else to indicate previous habitation. The kitchen was devoid of appliances. The sink faucet dripped; at least the water was still on. He was not certain about the electricity until Sylvie switched on the lamp on the end table.

A gesture with her sidearm bade the man seat himself in one of the armchairs. He had not spoken since the last of his questions in English. Who are you? Where are you taking me? Sylvie seated herself in the wooden chair. It squeaked a protest against her light frame. Langford took up a position between the man and the front door. What he would do should the man attempt to flee, he had no idea.

Sylvie said, in English, "I do not care to know your name, and wasting time protesting your innocence or ignorance annoys me. I do not care for the torture." She raised the Beretta. "I shall begin with the left foot and work my way up to the knee. Then with the right foot. I have the, what is it you say? The box of shells? So I—"

The pistol fired. It startled a cry from Langford, and a gasp of pain from the man. Blood began to well from his left foot. He leaned forward to examine the wound, and stopped when Sylvie shook her head and aimed the pistol at his nose. His pale skin spoke of anguish, and his pale eyes registered shock. Thick lips opened and closed as he gulped air.

"I am sorry," said Sylvie, although she sounded anything but. "It is the trigger. It has what is called the two-ounce pull. I might inadvertently empty the clip if I sneeze. *Eh bien*, let us proceed. You came for my companion. What is it that you think to do with him?"

"Please," said the man. "I am on warfarin. On blood thinner. For stroke. The bleeding may not stop."

Sylvie shrugged. "Then speak quickly."

"I-I... it was not supposed to be like this. A simple snatch, they said. Take him to the *Hauptbahnhof.* To the newsstand. They will do the rest. Please! I need to put pressure on this."

Already blood had welled up and over the sides of his brown leather shoes, to form a puddle on the rug. The cuffs of his brown trousers, long in the European fashion, were soaked.

"What do you mean by the rest?" asked Sylvie.

The man risked a glance at Langford. "He has a flash drive. They want it back. They also want to know whether he has discovered what is on it."

"What is on it?" asked Sylvie.

"I don't know." Panic set in as she took careful aim, this time at his ankle. "I don't know! I swear it! I wasn't told. They didn't tell me."

"Are your friends still at the train station?"

"I don't know. Maybe."

"How were you supposed to make the contact with them?"

He started to reach into his shirt pocket with both hands, and stopped, eyes wide with alarm. She made a little gesture of permission with the pistol. Carefully he extracted a folded piece of paper and offered it to her.

"I was to call this number if I encountered a difficulty."

Sylvie leaned closer and took it, and unfolded it one-handed. After a quick glance, she said, to Langford, "Your Palmetto."

He gave it to her. She placed it atop her right thigh and keyed it. Scant seconds later, they heard Montclair respond. Sylvie gave him a summary and the phone number on the paper.

"We have heard little that is useful," she told him. "He is bleeding, and claims the thinner. He may remain here. If he is stupid enough to run, let him bleed to death."

"One moment," said Montclair. The device went dead for almost two minutes. "I have set a response in motion," he broke back in. "It may or may not be successful."

"I wish to return to Brussels," Sylvie went on. "I have the better equipment there to work on the flash drive.

Evacuation by the helicopter from here would be quickest." She paused for a tender look at Langford. "We will both of us be coming."

Columbus, Ohio

The unexpected appearance of Lilac left Matt speechless. Wide-eyed, Newcombe gaped at her. His mouth worked as if he were trying to identify the taste of what he had just eaten. Lilac broke the stunned silence.

"We have to stop meeting like this," she said, to Matt. "The NSA is getting suspicious." She squinted in the dim light. "That looks remarkably like the President."

"How did *you* get in here?" Newcombe asked shakily.

She shrugged. "I didn't know there was any 'here' to get into. I simply pictured the person I wanted to be with. That would be Matt here." She looked around. "What is this, a gas reservoir?" She sniffed. "Ethanol reservoir."

"Lilac, what are you doing here?"

She gave him an arch look. "Well, I like that!" she said. "Maybe I should go back to California."

"No," Matt said quickly. "No... don't."

"Much better. Matt... why is he affixed to the wall?"

He brandished the key to the cuffs. "I was just about to release one of his hands and leave him to the rest when you showed up."

She looked glum. "I see. And then?"

He did not answer.

"You were going to leave him here?"

"Jesse," he reminded her.

She hung her head. She spoke softly, not looking up at him. "I understand, Matt. I would not dispute your choice. I think you have the right, for Jesse. But, my love—and yes, I do love you. You belong to Kerise, but you also belong to me. That is why you were drawn to me, that very first time. We are kindred spirits, you and I." She gestured toward Newcombe. "Matt, this is not you. You can argue that I don't know much about you, and that would be true. But I know enough to say that this does not become you. You are better than this. You are better than he is."

Matt heaved a great sigh, and nodded slowly. "I don't," he managed. "I don't." But he was unable to finish whatever it was that he didn't. Inside him poised a clot of stone where he should have had a heart. Guilt, perhaps, or shame, or the last vestiges of his anger and sorrow, fighting to live on. He shut his eyes, sealing himself inside. He turned over this and that in the hand of his mind, seeking answers, and stunned by the questions and revelations. Not before had he examined himself in this manner. Who was he supposed to be? What was he supposed to do? Jesse mattered—but what would Jesse want him to do? Matt needed, not forgiveness, but a recalibration of purpose.

His eyes unshuttered at the touch on his arm. "You can talk to me," whispered Lilac.

The words sank in. He heard his "Yeah," though he made no sound. A breath empowered him. "I have a room," he told her.

He disappeared with her, the shout of protest from the wall terminating abruptly from his ears.

French Lick, Indiana

Impatient, Frank Church raised Oliver West again, this time from the motel room he had taken. He had been instructed to phone West the following day, but with Hartland still in town, he concluded that he might need an edge, in the form of information. West had set a plan in motion; Church needed to know what it was.

Church heard a yawn at the other end. The words themselves were slurred, by sleep or by alcohol. "You're becoming tiresome, Frank. Just a moment."

Church heard clicking, followed by a steady but unobtrusive hum.

"Now we can talk freely," said West. "What's on your mind?"

"Hartland is too quiet."

"You worry too much. She's out in the cold now. I'm tempted to send a team for her."

"Jesus! She's not that dangerous."

West sighed through the phone. "Why have you called?"

"You mentioned bringing... *him* out in the open."

"So I did. Ever heard of *Kinderheim*?"

Church had to think for a moment. "Something like Save the Children?"

"Porter sponsors three through *Kinderheim*. We have two of them under surveillance. One in Sri Lanka, the other in Nicaragua."

Church nodded to himself. West had made a smart move indeed. But one more question had to be satisfied in order for the task to be successful. "How do you propose to notify Porter of this?"

West told him.

⁂

Columbus, Ohio

"This is where you're staying?" asked Lilac, giving the motel room a cursory once-over. The television was on at threshold volume, tuned to a news talk show. The ceiling fan still operated, gently washing the room with air. "Well... since the Feds have my camper, I suppose this will have to do. How's the bed?"

He gaped at her.

"Oh," she said. "No. I wouldn't object—I'd cooperate heartily—but it's not what you need right now." She patted the bedcover beside her. "Sit down."

Matt obeyed.

"Now talk to me."

He folded his hands together and clutched them between his knees as he hunched over.

"You can't breathe like that," she said. "Lean back. Give your lungs room to expand."

Again he obeyed, this time adding a little chuckle. Arms locked at the elbows supported him. "Yes, Doctor."

Lilac nodded approvingly. "Humor. That's good." She twisted a little to face him. "Matt... how long have you... known?"

He thought back, and shook his head. "I've been able to do odd things for as long as I can remember," he said slowly, finding his way. "For a long time I didn't think anything of it, and nothing I did was ostentatious. Maybe picking up a dropped spoon in the kitchen. That sort of thing."

"Been there."

"I-I stole a candy bar, once, to see if I could do it. I ate it, but it didn't taste very good."

"Guilt has a terrible taste. I tried an ice cream bar. I just looked at it. It melted."

"Yeah. I suppose I would have made a great bank robber. Instead, I settled for the Crime of the Millennium, didn't I?" It wasn't a question.

"It would be, if news of it ever got out. The White House dares not acknowledge it. It's probably the best-kept secret among the D.C. security acronyms. But they're looking now. Not just for you, Matt. For *all* of us."

He frowned. "How many of us are there?"

"I don't know. I can sense about half a dozen? It's hard to tell. And it's not like we talk."

"I know of one other," he said, thinking of Analou. "Well, two, but one's dead. They killed him."

The tip of her tongue moistened her lips, and he knew she was about to say something he might not want to hear. He held his breath.

"May I...be heard?" she asked.

He nodded, unable to deny her.

She rushed her words, as if she were afraid he might break into them. "You want to avenge your brother, and you've every right to. The difference between you and everyone else who has lost a loved one to a senseless war caused by leaders and politicians is that you possess the means as well as the desire to take revenge. In all those other instances, those officials can laugh off such desires for vengeance, such protests, because they know people are impotent. They know they themselves are very safe.

"So look at what you've done, Matt. You've shown the Very-Safe that they are not so safe after all. And because of the way you can get at them, they'll never know when or from where you'll strike. Their necks will have perpetual cricks from always looking over their shoulders. Their fear will lead to tics and twitches. From this moment on, they'll know there's someone out there who can come for them and hold them accountable. Your abduction of the President has changed the game, forever.

"And it's not just here, in this country. Word will get out. Every political leader everywhere, and all of the Very-Safe, the powers behind the thrones, will know what can happen to them if they try to rule instead of govern."

"How?" Matt asked, dubious. "How would word get out? Who would believe it?"

"Oh, Matt." She sighed patiently. "Washington is a sieve. It's a faucet without that little rubber thingie. It's a hose that the dog got to. Okay, yes, our existence will be classified beyond belief. But there will be someone who has a friend in London, or Paris, or Beijing, or New Delhi. The classification will be downgraded to 'You didn't hear this from me, but I have it on confirmed authority that.' In a way, we'll be like the X-Men, except that we're real."

She sobered, and went on. "We'll be hunted down. Top priority will be given to finding the means of controlling us, of compelling us to do their bidding. Of weaponizing us. Failing that—and they almost certainly will fail—we'll be killed."

Matt swallowed hard, unable to credit the words that were coming to him. "So...you're saying...now that I've made my point, I should just let him go."

The smile in her eyes held a sun's warmth for him. That on her lips was colder than outer space.

"Not even that," she said. "Just tell them where he is."

He fell back on the bed and stared up at the ceiling. At the fan with one of its four blades missing. Still it rotated evenly. That signified something to him. He tried to puzzle out what it was.

"Yick," said Lilac. "I've been in these clothes for a dance or two. I should have brought some with me."

"We can shop later," he said absently, still adrift.

She stood up. "Mind if I use your shower?"

He nodded, and realized it was the wrong gesture in context. "No, go right ahead."

He closed his eyes to the sounds of her disrobing. The rustle of fabric as the jersey was drawn over her head. The zipper of her jeans. No thump of shoes, for she was barefoot. A snap of elastic. Presently he heard the brittle hiss of water striking the floor of the shower. The sound softened, and he knew she had gotten in. A moment or two later, the brittleness returned.

"Hey."

He rolled over to look at her. Water beaded and dripped from her as she stood in the doorway to the bathroom, feet apart, one hand on her hip, the other covered with a white motel washcloth.

Words fled him.

"Do you happen to have any real soap?" she asked. "All I can find are these motel samplers."

He was on the verge of responding when a puff of displaced air wafted over him. He turned his head toward the source of it, and found Kerise.

Alexandria, Virginia

Lieutenant Colonel Rother held his Palmetto away and glared at it as if it had just given him unforgivable offense. "Where the hell are you?" he yelled.

"Far away," Teague said again. "Al, that's all I can tell you."

Rother turned to gaze out the side window of his Land Rover. He had parked in a Walmart lot because it was an easy location for him to determine whether he was being followed. As far as he could tell, he was not, but that meant nothing in the age of surveillance drones the size of sparrows. The sparrows, in turn, if they located him, could send a signal to a Predator 3 armed with precision missiles that could take out himself and his vehicle with minimal collateral damage. Mentally Rother crossed his fingers, and watched people get out of or into vehicles. No one seemed to have the slightest interest in him. Cars pulled into the lot and sought the closest places to the front door, so that the shoppers wouldn't have so far to walk. Lazy, he thought.

"I suppose I shouldn't ask you how you got there," he said to Teague.

"That would be best."

Rother gave himself a little nod as he finally made up his mind. He had already crossed his Rubicon. "Have you seen the papers?"

Hesitation at the other end made Rother sit up straight. Knowing in advance what Teague was about to ask, he said, "Yes, I'm probably being monitored. I can't worry about that now. What's done is done, and I wouldn't retract what I wrote, even if I could. What I need is—"

"Yeah," Teague broke in. "You do. Are you sure you want it?"

"I've already crossed one Rubicon. What's one more?"

"Understood. Do you remember where we kept Kuznetsov before we turned him over?"

Rother shook his head, even though Teague could not see it. "They put in a park across the street. The place is not secure."

"That won't matter. I'm doubly positive. No worries. I'll be there in a second. We'll work it out from that point."

Teague rang off before Rother could respond. He slumped back in his seat, and rubbed his eyes. Teague was coming from far away, and all flights had been cancelled, all commercial aircraft grounded. Rother had a vague idea of Teague's location; if the rogue agent had his own F-35 with stealth technology, he might make it in a couple hours. Otherwise, a meeting was impossible. Yet Teague had sounded confident.

How?

With no other option, Rother began a circuitous drive toward the park in question, his eyes on the traffic and above the traffic.

027

Brussels, Belgium

For the fifth time Langford fingered the guest badge that Montclair had arranged for him. Pinned to the left pocket of his shirt, it displayed his name and photograph and security status, which consisted of a bright red numeral 1. He had not been told what the number signified, nor had he inquired. As long as he was kept in the loop regarding the flash drive and the efforts to decode it, he was happy.

It had astonished him to learn that Sylvie resided in the Interpol Headquarters itself. Clearly she lived for her work. While she might indulge in a rare overnight liaison, she was always on call. For reasons still unexplained, she had taken to him. Even Montclair gave him a few small signs of deference and acceptance. Apparently Sylvie's belief in him spoke volumes in a language he did not understand.

Fresh clothing for him had already been delivered to her quarters by the time they arrived. Following a shower and shave, he had dressed in a dark blue suit off the rack, but one which fitted him well. Sylvie, in simple blue slacks and jersey, approved him with just a look. He in turn eyed her with a measure of askance.

"I thought you would be more comfortable," she told him, explaining his attire. "*Moi*, I am always the casual. *C'est plus facile...*" She came to a stop and made a face. "It is more easy for me to move quickly if there is need."

"*Je parle français*," he reminded her.

Her only response was a faint smile.

Now, recalling that, he shook his head ruefully. He'd had a year of high school French, and later the occasional practice in a bistro, ordering a drink or asking for directions to the WC. Learn the important words first. His German was far better.

She emerged from her office workroom to make a face at him, a sign that she had yet to be successful in decoding the text on the flash drive. She opened the door to a box of dark hardwood on a stand by the window, to reveal two or three bottles and a couple of crystal tumblers. After pouring two fingers of Gran Duque de Alba brandy into each tumbler, she brought one to Langford, and sat down beside him on the sofa. A mild toast preceded sips.

The tumblers, he noted, were Waterfords, and the brandy of high quality. He was unaccustomed to such indulgence. His gaze went to the window that gave onto the avenue four levels below. In the park across the way, the tops of trees swayed with the early evening breeze. Were it not for the flash drive that evidently was worth killing for, and that at least one man had died for, the atmosphere might have been romantic, except for the Beretta clipped over her left hip. Even so, Langford savored the moment, waiting for Sylvie to bring him back to reality.

She was silent. She was leaning back on a cushion, one knee over the other, her left arm laid along the arm of the sofa with her fingers curled around her drink, her right arm along the back of the sofa, hand and forearm behind him. He glanced at her, and could not stop himself from seeing her as a woman. He had seen—he had *touched*—what the clothing concealed: the slender frame, the petite breasts, the wiry legs, the—

Langford shook himself. She's an Interpol operative, ran his thoughts, trained and dangerous and brilliant in her chosen field. I'm a reporter. Only the flash drive makes me important.

He looked away.

"It is a difficult and complicated life for the lovers," she said, her voice barely audible. She fortified herself with another sip or two. "I do the office work, yes, but some of the times I work in the field. It is that some of the times I must... do the things that my lover..."

"You mean like that man who broke into our room," he said, filling in her blank. "You mean kill."

Slowly she shook her head. "My lover would accept that of me." She barked a laugh and added, "Like the spy movies, *n'est-ce pas*? *Mais non*, it is that I... what I must do is regarded as…" She paused, clearly struggling for the right word. She settled on, "Unfaithful. *Entendu*? This is not good for the relationship, you see. It is so therefore that I must not have one."

"So therefore."

"*Oui*," she said sadly. "*Alors*, the hours. I have spent the nights in here, to work on the problem, to sleep on the sofa, to live on the coffee and the cigarettes and the brandy, until I have the solution. This is too not good for the relationship."

"No, I suppose not."

"*Eh bien*, Evan," she pronounced it Yvonne, "I have found the key to open the text. It is the date key. But I do not have the hole in which to insert the key."

"Yet."

She smiled. "*Oui*. Yet. *Encore*."

"And now you take a break from the work."

"A break? Ah, *oui*, the break. Yes."

"So you eat here and drink here," Langford went on. "And you work here, of course. And you sleep here."

Sylvie grimaced, and nodded. "*C'est vrai*."

Langford set his tumbler on the end table. "Perhaps there is something you have not done here, yet… *encore*."

She held his gaze for a long moment, and finally gave a tiny nod. "Please to lock the door," she said.

⁂

Columbus, Ohio

The only sounds in the room were the spray of water in the shower and Matt's beating heart, now stiff as stone. They seemed to go on for hours, though they could occupy but a few seconds. To Matt it seemed as if no one were brave enough to speak first. Certainly he could not; he had no idea what he might possibly say. An unexpected hard tug at his pants leg startled Matt and raced his heart. The words from Kerise stunned him.

"I leave you alone for two minutes," she fairly shouted. "*Two minutes*."

Matt could not help laughing.

Kerise walked past the bed toward the shower. The girl

167

there did not shrink back, but stood calmly, waiting. Kerise gave her a slow inspection, from face to toes and back to face, and followed this with a slow nod.

"You, too, Kerise?" asked Lilac.

Kerise's face betrayed no astonishment. "So he told you about me," she said pleasantly. "But... no, you are asking me something else. My answer is no, I am not like you. I had an assist to this place from someone who is. You are... Nuala Lowry."

She held out her wet free hand. "Call me Lilac."

Kerise took it, and introduced herself.

"Of the French aircraft Renauds?" asked Lilac. The expression on Kerise's face pushed her to explain. "My father used to work for General Dynamics in San Diego. Your family had some business with them."

Kerise's mouth worked. Finally she said, "Aren't you a little chilly?"

"Now that you mention it." Lilac returned to the shower. "Be right with you."

Matt could only stare at Kerise in wonder as she returned to the bed. To his surprise, she stretched out on her stomach beside him. "Awkward, *n'est-ce pas*?" she chuckled.

"Kerise—"

She covered his mouth with her hand. "I am sure there is a story behind all this. I wish to hear it. I like her. But I came here because," she lowered her voice, "Matt, I know what you have done."

"So does she."

"It's not that I don't fault you for it— She does?"

He rolled to face her, resting his cheek on his arm. "It's complicated."

"At the moment, it is very French. But we can work that out that later. A time-share arrangement, or something. Matt, this has caused us trouble... and while I understand... oh, my love, if something were to happen to you, I too would want to find whoever did it and... and... but this is not you, what you have done. You are better than this."

Matt's eyes closed. "She told me that, too," he whispered.

"I like her."

"Yes, you said."

Her face blurred for him, as if he were looking at her through a rainy window. It took him a moment to realize that he was crying. It had all gone wrong, and yet it was all right. Jesse had been avenged. It was not necessary to kill his killer; Matt had given him the fright of his life, one that would last and affect him for the remainder of his life. Carl Newcombe would never recover; he was permanently-damaged goods. Matt saw now how he could add a ferocious embarrassment to the punishment. At the same time, his actions had jeopardized Kerise's project. Somehow, he had to make up for it.

"Once they have the President back, they'll lift the flight restrictions," he said, as much to himself as to her. "But I'm sure they'll intensify the search for me and the others. The people in the government who know of our existence will now inform and warn the security services. They'll redouble their efforts. We can hide for only so long. I'm known; so is Analou." He glanced toward the shower. "Are there any more besides her?"

"Two others that I know of. And yes, the search will intensify. Your abduction of the President has shown the government just how vulnerable it is to you and your, ah, kind."

Matt winced. "Kerise, I'm just like you. We're just like you."

"Oh, I know." She touched his arm. The contact warmed him. "You have an ability that few others possess. Others have abilities that you do not possess. We are all each of us good at something—painting, math, fingernail decoration, keeping files straight. But your ability, and Nuala's, and Analou's are needed. It is not too great a statement to say that they are needed to save us."

"I quite agree," said Lilac, striding across the room toward them now. She was wearing a white terrycloth bathrobe, and had some clothing draped over her arm. She plucked at the robe. "Sorry it took so long. I just stepped out to get this and a couple other items. The clerk was...a little gaga."

"Can't imagine why," said Matt.

Lilac dumped the loose clothing on the bed, and stretched out on the other side of him. "Well, this is cozy." For a long and silent moment she eyed Kerise up and down. Finally she said, "So you're the competition."

"Meow."

Lilac laughed. "But no. Our world is brave and new, with rules written by ourselves."

"I agree," Kerise said immediately. "Provided that Matt is willing."

He frowned. "To do what?"

They just looked at him.

His "Oh!" was a burst of air. His lips moved, but no sounds emerged. Presently he found some words. "I can barely handle one of you."

"We'll be gentle," Kerise assured him, and it was settled.

Another long silence followed. For the umpteenth time Matt found himself wondering what the hell he was doing. Over but a few days, so much had changed, irrevocably so. He needed to adjust, to catch up. Glances at the women to either side of him told him he would have help.

But a woman, a friend, was also missing. "Where's Analou?" he asked.

"It turns out she can do transfers," Kerise answered. "That's how I got here. But she doesn't know how to accompany them."

"We need a *Paranormal Handbook*," grumbled Lilac. "Or *Transference for Dummies. Spoonwarping for Fun and Profit.*"

"And Teague?" asked Matt.

Kerise's tone revealed disappointment. "She sent him to rescue an old colleague of his," she explained. "Apparently the man blew the whistle on the government's tardy response to the restaurant bombings. Their initial incredulity cost lives, maybe thousands of them, so of course they wanted to cover their asses. Now," she finished, and rolled to face Lilac, "how did you two meet?"

Lilac told her, omitting nothing, although at one point she hesitated in her narrative. When she was done, Kerise said, "You sensed him. That's why you were in La Jolla. Something he gives off—and I don't mean pheromones—

alerted you to him. You can detect others, can't you?"

Slowly Lilac nodded. "It's very faint," she said. "I can concentrate if I detect a whiff." A bright smile transformed her face into that of a gamine imp. "Think of it as passing neural gas."

Kerise swallowed a hiccup. Matt hushed them both. He was staring, frowning, at the television set. A mad search for the remote turned it up on the floor. He snatched it, dropped it, and got it back, turning up the sound.

"...Trincomalee, on the coast," the newscaster was saying. "They have identified themselves as agents of Homeland Security, but it was not clear why the girl was taken. Other agents have taken a schoolboy in Nicaragua, and have flown him to Panama, again without official statement. Homeland Security has denied any involvement in these abductions, and for the moment officials regard them as the actions of a rogue faction within the department, whose true purposes remain hidden. Anyone with any information that might help to clarify these events is asked to call the number at the bottom of the screen." He paused, glanced briefly to one side, and added, "We'll be back after this message."

"That's got to be that girl," gasped Kerise. "Rema... Manorema. Which means the boy would be—"

"Miguel Dario," said Matt. His lips tightened and paled. "*Damn* them!"

"What is it?" worried Lilac. "What's happened?"

"He sponsors children through *Kinderheim*," Kerise told her. "Two of them have been taken hostage by our government."

"Veronique Ladama," said Matt. "She's in Senegal. They may not have gotten to her yet."

"You can't be sure," Kerise said. "Information from Africa is often spotty, and suspect."

"Kerise," said Matt, with finality. "I have to rescue them. There's no one else to do it."

Lilac cleared her throat for attention. "I'll need a photograph," she said.

028

Ohio, west of Columbus

The key, thought Geneva Hartland, driving east on Interstate 70, had to be in Columbus. Whatever Matthew Porter was up to, it was going to happen there. Her certainty overwhelmed the scarcity of evidence she had for this assessment. That Porter had been reported in Columbus did not mean he was still there now. But the only way she could return to the good graces of Echelon, and perhaps oust the treacherous Oliver West, was to locate Porter and spearhead his entrapment and capture.

Traffic was light just past the morning rush hour from Indianapolis, and the most dangerous obstacles to travel were the fragments of truck tires that littered the pavement. Even the car drivers, usually eager to show their Speedway skills, seemed to be moving at a pedestrian seventy-five to eighty miles an hour, or just five to ten over the speed limit. Hartland drove at just below the legal limit of seventy, which compelled almost everyone else to pass her, but at least she avoided being pulled over by the highway patrol...and identified. Almost certainly Oliver West and Frank Church had issued APBs for her.

Her vehicle, a Dodge Caliber, was a rental, but its accessories included GPS, smart phone, and voice-activated search capability. Accordingly, she accessed a holographic street map of Columbus and requested the location of the store where Porter had purchased the flashing and lighter fluid. It seemed to her likely that Porter had known the location of the store, which meant that he had seen it at some point. Pursuing this line of thought, she concluded that he must be staying in the general area.

A Subaru swerved around her, following too close and cutting back in too close, and Hartland gasped in shock and fear. Had she been located already? But the vehicle sped on, and gradually she relaxed. A question had been coalescing in her mind; she gave it words and broached it to the car's computer. Assuming a radius of ten city blocks, she requested the locations of all the motels in that area.

There were three.

She grimly nodded to herself, and pressed on the accelerator to keep up with the rest of the traffic.

⁓

Washington, D.C.

Despite the incontrovertible evidence of his own eyes, Teague still did not grasp how paranormal travel or telekinesis was possible. In this particular instance, it almost wasn't. An image of the intended destination was required—one of the arcane rules of paranormalness, he snorted. He'd had nothing; certainly no photographs of the safe house. Nor did he possess a photograph of Al Rother. Describing the house, or the park across the street, was insufficient. Rules!

Finally, however, he'd had an inspiration. A street sign post, the city, and a red neon light that read DAVEY'S TAV RN. The E, as far as Teague could recall, had never lit. The sprite of a girl named Analou had thought it might be sufficient. Teague crossed his fingers and hoped that the colors of the street signs had not changed in the interim.

They hadn't.

As on previous occasions, he wobbled a bit when he arrived in front of the tavern. Inside, a couple of men stared at him as if he had just materialized out of nowhere, which he had. They then peered into their mugs, frowned, and shrugged. Outside, Teague laughed lightly before proceeding down Gilmore to the next block, and the park across the street.

He walked slowly, surveying his surroundings without appearing to do so. If Rother had been tailed, there might be surveillance in the area. At the next intersection, he made for a park bench, where he sat down unobtrusively and gazed at the old brick and wood, two-story former dwelling, now with a real estate sign posted in the front yard. Someone had trimmed the grass recently, and pruned the shrubs, including deadheading a bank of lilacs so they would bloom the next year. Whether the place was still a safe house, or was up for legitimate sale, Teague could not determine. But the light in the second floor dormer window had not been turned on, which mean that Rother had yet to arrive.

Unable to remain in one place for too long, lest he be noticed, Teague got up and began to walk around the park, pausing here and there as if in appreciation of some flower or shrub. A squirrel darted unexpectedly across his path, startling him, and he realized he had become too tightly wound. His innate sense of impending danger remained at rest; gradually the tension eased from his body, and he allowed his shoulders to slump. He looked around, then, seemingly at random, until his gaze settled on the safe house, just visible through the foliage of a lilac. Right, then.

Teague returned to the bench. The dormer light was still off. But something had changed. It took him a few precious seconds to grasp what it was: an innocuous beige sedan was parked just down the street. It fairly screamed surveillance. Perched in the front seat were two men poring over what looked like a road atlas. Teague's fingers closed around the butt of his Sig Sauer. Were the men here for Rother, or for himself?

Upon a brief reflection, the answer came to him. The safe house itself was ultra-secure; only if Rother had been captured and made to talk, would the men have known about it. Therefore...

Teague eased back toward the shrubbery, torn between confirming Rother's situation and avoiding risk to himself. In the end, there was no help for it: he might hide for a time in the city, but he had no way of getting back to Kerise. From half a block away, he did not recognize the two men in the car, but surely they would recognize him, for he had traveled undisguised. An approach from the rear seemed the best option.

First, however, Teague had to determine whether the surveillance consisted of only one vehicle, and only one team.

Keeping deep within the park, Teague wandered around some more, this time with his attention focused on the surrounding four streets. Aside from the beige vehicle, nothing struck him as being out of place. A few kids played in front yards; a dog curled a muzzle to worry at an insect; a few bits of trash—candy wrappers and fast-food bags, mostly—fluttered in the intermittent breeze. But his danger sense was beginning to itch. He could find nothing with which to scratch it.

A flash of eureka galvanized him. That was it! Swiftly he looked all around. *There was nobody else in the park!* This late in the afternoon, there surely would be someone. An old geezer feeding peanuts to squirrels and popcorn to birds. A kid chasing a ball. *Someone!*

Even as he turned away from a large oak, he knew he had made a mistake. Now the only question was of survival. As long as he remained alive, he had a chance to avenge Lydia and the boys.

The pistol thrust against the middle of his back told Teague that his assailant was an idiot, but he let it go. The voice, when he heard it, stunned him—because he recognized it.

⚓

Columbus, Ohio

While Lilac looked on, Kerise was trying to caution Matt. "They don't expect you to contact them," she argued. "They believe you'll come after the children. They're prepared for that. They'll take you."

"If they can," Matt said dismissively. He checked the .45 pistol he had just stolen from a gunshop.

"This is not about the children," she went on. "This is about you. *You* are the resource, the pot of gold, the... the..."

He smiled. "I get what you're saying."

"Not completely. With Manorema, maybe you have a chance. You can transfer there, but well away from that school, based on the photograph. But what about Miguel? All you have is a head shot of him. The same is true of Veronique. If you materialize next to them, that's precisely where HomeSec will be. They're *expecting* you. They're *ready.*"

"Exactly," said Lilac.

They turned to look at her, as if they had forgotten that she was there.

"They're expecting *you*, Matt," she explained. "They're not expecting *us*."

The response stunned them. Kerise could only stare blankly at her. Matt nodded slowly. "Good point," he conceded. With a grin at Kerise, he added, "Now aren't you glad I brought a weapon for you?"

Kerise relented. "So where to?"

"It's dark in Trincomalee and Senegal," answered Matt. "So Nicaragua."

"Um..." said Lilac, and laid her pistol on the bed.

Matt frowned at her.

"Nicaragua," she repeated.

"That's where Miguel Dario lives."

Lilac's lips puffed out with her sigh. "Yes. And the Nicaragua government would poop bricks before allowing Homeland Security to send a few agents into their country."

Matt sat down hard on the bed, and swore softly. Presently he gave himself a tiny nod. "Fake news," he said. "They staged it to bring me out." Relief swept him. But a difficulty remained. He looked up, at Kerise, at Lilac. Their eyes shone back at him, filled with anticipation. This was his call; he supported the three children.

His voice was low, almost inaudible, and as soon as he started speaking, Kerise and Lilac sat down on the bed, bracketing him.

"There's no way to be certain of our circumstances," he began. "Let's suppose they're waiting for me to call. The phone will be tapped, of course. Normally it takes half a minute or so to trace my phone, but these people have access to high-tech, and can probably locate me within five, ten seconds. What they *can't* do is send a team to pick me up once they know where I am, because they simply cannot move that fast." He felt his face darken. "But they don't have to. They can summon the local police. They'll try to keep me on the line long enough. Damn damn damn."

"You're missing the point, Matt," Lilac said roughly.

"Calling that number is not relevant."

"If I *don't* call, they *will* go after the kids."

"Not if we get them first," Kerise put in, keeping to Lilac's point. "Let's stick to your original plan. Get the kids out, and damn HomeSec and the lot of them."

A sound—a scrape from outside—alerted Matt, but it was already too late. The door burst open from a hand-held police battering ram, and a chunky, gray-haired woman in her late fifties stepped into the room, holding a Glock .41. For just a moment, Matt was too startled to transfer, but that moment was all the woman needed.

"Uh-uh," she said, addressing him, but aiming at Kerise. "If you leave, I'll shoot whoever remains behind."

The uniformed policeman behind her said, "Ma'am, I can't let you do that."

"It's all right, officer," said the woman, without turning around. "I won't have to do that. Will I, Matthew Porter?"

Brussels, Belgium

Again Langford found himself contemplating the life led by Sylvie Dubray. Only hours ago had he learned her last name. She had looked at him curiously when she had said it, as if it were supposed to strike a chord with him. He had wondered at the time whether that was her true last name, but not for long. The woman was far more important to him than the name.

She was and had been in her workshop for close to three hours now, and it was almost time for lunch. As she had been two hours late for dinner the previous evening, it seemed likely she would forego the break for sustenance. He glanced at the basket of petite baguettes and the plate of butter on the coffee table, and considered whether to take something in to her. But her workshop was sacro-sanct. She had not said this in so many words, but he had determined it from the way she closed the door, sealing herself off from the rest of the Solar System.

She was right in what she had told him yesterday: hers was no life for sharing. He hated to admit that to himself.

The keyboard on his laptop had rested idle for too

many minutes. He needed to file a column. First, however, he had to compose it. He typed a few words cautiously, uncertain of his subject matter. Everything that had transpired since the brief encounter in the Munich Zoo with the smuggler known as Chartreuse was classified to one extent or another.

A cry from the workshop brought Langford to his feet. As he hurried to the door, it opened, and a weary but happy Sylvie greeted him as if she had known he would be standing there. Her short dark hair had been tugged on from time to time, probably in frustration, and her eyes were red from looking too long at fine details on a monitor.

"*Le jeu est fait,*" she breathed into his chest.

"You found the key?"

She nodded against him. "I read and heard... oh, *c'est incroyable*! I will tell you..."

She slipped past him and made for the sofa, where she flopped down and sprawled. "I would like the coffee. Would you please?" She held up her hands for inspection. "I am the tremble."

Langford sat down beside her and poured. "Perhaps I should hold the cup while you sip."

"*Mais non, je ne veux pas de café.* I want...oh, I do not know what it is that I want." She regarded him with eyes that were softening, now only pink, and touched his arm. Her hand sent a jolt of warmth through him, though it was cool and dry. "You are patient with me."

Sylvie got up and walked unsteadily to the window. Nose pressed against the glass, she stared off into space, and seemed not to notice when Langford joined her there. Her breath cast a light splotch on the window. He kept silent, letting her find her own way.

"It is all changed," she said at last, not looking at him. "All the things that we have done, they will go on in vain. Evan... I do not want no longer these things."

"Sylvie..."

She turned to him and smiled. "I know it is that you do not know what it is I am talking about," she said. "I will tell you." She held out her hand. "Come with me to the sofa. We will sit, and we will talk. And then...and then I am frightened."

The word shook Langford. If whatever was on that disk scared Sylvie, it would probably turn the blood in his veins to ice. He kissed her softly on the lips, drawing strength from her.

"*Oui*," she said. "We shall do that there, too."

⁂

Washington, D.C.

"Rother," said Teague.

"I'm sorry about this," said the Army officer. "I am. But they said my slate would be wiped clean, and that I would be allowed to retire on full pension."

The barrel of the pistol still pressed against his spine. "And you believed them."

"I don't want to hear it," Rother said gruffly. "Right now we're going over to that beige sedan you had your eye on a few moments ago. They'll take it from there, and I'll be home free."

"Get me let you out of here," said Teague. "Come with me."

Rother nudged him with the pistol. "Start walking."

Teague spun, his arm sweeping the pistol aside. It went off, but he grabbed it and shoved the slide back before removing it from Rother. The officer swore, and shook his injured hand.

"Al, you always were an amateur," Teague said, stepping back a couple of paces. He glanced at the sedan. Neither occupant seemed to have observed the reversal of fortunes. "I'm disappointed," he said, as he motioned Rother ahead of him. They began making their way toward the northeast corner and the bus stop there. "I could have gotten you away, where they would never have found you. Now, I can't trust you. No matter what you'd tell me, I wouldn't be able to believe it. You don't know it yet, and you won't for a lile whonger, but you've just screwed yourself royally. Hop stere."

Rother obeyed, looking up. "It's a tree."

"Turn around."

"What are you—"

"Furn the tuck around!"

Rother did so. Teague whacked him across the back of the head with the barrel of Rother's pistol, then tossed the firearm onto his body after he fell. The tree blocked the view from the sedan.

Moments later, Teague was heading back into downtown Washington.

***

Columbus, Ohio

"All of you, stay seated," ordered Hartland. "Hands where I can see them." She eyed Lilac first, then Kerise. "Who are you?" she asked the redhead.

"No one of consequence to you," Kerise answered calmly.

"I didn't ask you that, young lady," snapped Hartland. "I asked you who the fuck you were."

Her tone did not change. "And I have given you the only response you're going to get."

"I can shoot you right now."

Lilac smiled. "Not really, no, you can't."

Hartland glared at her. "Let's try you, then. Who are you?"

"My name would mean nothing to you."

"I gather this isn't going well," Matt said to Hartland.

"Shut up."

"Something has gone wrong for you," Lilac went on. "What is it? You've... ah, you've lost your job, and with it your power, position, and prestige. Oooh, dear." She barked a laugh. "And you're hoping that by turning Matt over to the government, you'll regain favor and position."

"Who *are* you?"

"That is a very silly question, Doctor Hartland."

Hartland's jaw dropped, and she took a step back. "You—you're one of them."

"Are they under arrest, Doctor Hartland," asked the policeman. He was standing in the open doorway, one hand clutching zipstrips. "We have better places at headquarters for you to conduct interviews."

Hartland did not turn around. "I, ah, no. No, that won't be necessary. I can handle this from here."

"You're sure?"

"You've done your job, officer," she said firmly. "Now it's time for me to do mine. As soon as air travel restrictions are lifted, someone from my department will be in touch with your chief."

Backing up, Hartland eased the door shut after the officer departed.

"We can't help you," said Lilac. "Not with Echelon. And after this, you'll be in disfavor for other administrative positions. Even if you were able to turn Matthew and myself over to Echelon... ah, or to this Frank Church, you're out." She made a little gesture. "Go ahead. Pull the trigger. See what happens."

"What? No!"

Hartland's hand trembled. She seemed unable to pull the weapon back, or to aim it elsewhere. Her index finger tightened on the trigger. She struggled against it, her face white with effort. Matt heard a click as the hammer fell on the firing chamber. Nothing else happened.

"Look in your purse," suggested Lilac.

Hartland dipped her free hand, and came up with several loose bullets.

"*Now* you tell me," Matt growled.

Lilac looked contrite. "Sorry." To Hartland, she said, "You're not shooting anyone. You're not taking us any-where. And you've nowhere else to go, Doctor Hartland."

Hartland slumped against the door. The pistol spilled from her hand and landed on the carpet. Matt found himself beginning to feel sorry for her. He shook his head hard to clear it.

"Me, too," said Lilac, beside him. "What do you want to do with her?"

Matt's eyes widened. "Me?"

"It's your honor," she pointed out. "She came here for you."

"Lilac," he said, "what kind of person is she?"

Lilac was silent for a few moments. Hartland looked as if she had a headache. Kerise sat very quietly, as if she were about to learn something.

"She's good at what she does," Lilac decided. "And that's administration and office management. She has some flaws, as do we all. Maybe she's learned something from all this." She turned to him. "It's still your call, Matt."

Suddenly he grinned. "Got an idea."

029

On the east coast of Sri Lanka, northwest of Trincomalee

Despite some trepidation, Matt and Kerise encountered no difficulties when they arrived at the devastated coastal village where lived Manorema Kulasingam, the adolescent girl whom he supported through *Kinderheim*. He tucked the pistol back under his belt and breathed a little sigh of relief.

"It's dawn," Kerise noted, unnecessarily, for already a chord of the orange-red sun had emerged above the line of the horizon. The sky above it was clear; there would be no rain today.

She followed Matt up from the beach and into the unnamed village. They were looking for a hut with the front of the thatch roof bashed down and with a clutch of three palm trees in front, next to the stream of dried mud that passed for a street. A white and brown dog of terrier ancestry yapped at them as they passed, and yapped even louder when Kerise stopped to look at him. People were already up and about, preparing for the day as people in the village had done for tens of thousands of days. Life, no matter how hard and base, went on.

Kerise heard three chimes of a bell of thin metal—a signal of some sort. She caught up Matt and gave him a questioning look.

"The children all walk together to school," he explained. "They have half an hour to dress, eat, and assemble." He looked around. "No Westerners but us have been here. HomeSec was never here."

"I thought as much."

Suddenly he pointed. "There!"

The hut matched the description Manorema had given Matt in one of her translated letters. The girl did speak enough English—Sri Lanka had once been called Ceylon, and had been under British control for more than a century—but wrote in the language in which she was comfortable.

"Do you speak any Tamil?" asked Kerise.

"Some nouns and verbs," he replied. "Nothing to write home about." He paused, keening an ear.

"Something?"

"Helicopter. Very faint." He began to hasten toward the hut, with Kerise barely keeping up. "Rema," he called out, urgently.

In the hut, nothing moved, or made a sound. Running now, he called again. As he reached the doorway, with Kerise right behind him, a girl stepped into view. The top of her head reached Matt's shoulder. She was dressed in an old tangerine sari and burnt orange camisole. A red bindi seemed to glow on her forehead. Glowing dark eyes regarding him, at first with astonishment, then with curiosity.

"Matthew?" she said, as if it were the first time she had spoken the word aloud.

He froze. Manorema looked about to rush to him in sheer joy. He was unprepared for the lovely reality of her. Heretofore she had been the object of a photograph. Of numerous photographs. Of movements in her dances. Of pitiful meals of rice and vegetables that he sent extra money to augment. Of her drawing something as she sat on the rickety cot that served as her bed and sofa. Now she was here before him, dark and exotic, her eyes reflecting the smile on her lips.

Breathless, she asked, "Have you come for me?"

"Save your speech, bucko," said Kerise, now standing beside him. "She needs no persuasion."

"Rema, pack your things quickly," said Matt. "We have to leave now."

The girl nodded, and rushed off. Presently her mother appeared, attired in a dirty white shift that reached below her knees. A somber expression clouded her eyes. Tears were imminent. She spoke in a language that was both harsh and melodic.

Kerise looked at him. He said, "She wants to know if Rema will be safe with me. In this context, she means will I take care of her and see her to a better life." Returning his attention to the woman, he pressed his hands together and gave her a little bow. She did not speak his language, but she smiled faintly at what he told her. When he was done, she clasped his hands in hers and shook them. A sigh punctuated her gratitude.

Manorema returned, carrying an old canvas bag about half-full. Eyes wet, she hugged her mother, and looked questioningly at Matt. After a final smile for her mother, he reached for Manorema's hand, and she yielded it to him readily. "Over to the banyan tree," he said to Kerise. "I don't want anyone to see this."

"Let's go home," she said, to the girl.

The whup-whup sounds grew louder. As they reached the banyan, the helicopter settled down on the sparse grass between the village and the beach, and several men and women in camouflage fatigues rushed out. Almost immediately they spotted Matt and his companions. Still running, they aimed their rifles and yelled incoherent orders.

"Matthew?" whimpered Manorema.

Orders were shouted; Matt paid them no mind. Only the girl and the woman at his side mattered. But the arrival of the men said that he was running out of time. There remained one *Kinderheim* child unaccounted for.

The approaching men were aiming their weapons now—but not at him. He understood the tactic. A transfer by himself alone at this moment would endanger Kerise and Manorema. But if he took them to Nicaragua without knowing the situation on the ground there, they might be in more danger.

A deep breath calmed his heart. He had no choice, not now. But in the moment of transfer, he heard small arms fire.

⁂

eastern Senegal

In a nameless collection of rude huts deep into Senegal, Nuala "Lilac" Lowry suffered the stares of dark eyes as she made her way along the quagmire of a path, the result of a downpour a few hours earlier. No one spoke, and even if they had, she doubted she would understand it. She sensed, rather than saw, hostility.

Thick, humid air rendered their features like an Impressionist's painting. She had used the image of the hamlet's gardens to telekine herself, rather than the unclear image of the girl. Entering the hamlet itself, she noticed that the hut ahead had a cross atop the thatch roof, and she gazed at it with wondering eyes. A church here? She walked faster now. Perhaps the priest or minister knew a Western language. If all else failed, she could try transmitting mental images.

The irregular sounds of approaching vehicles began to reach her ears. Motors revved and idled, as if the drivers were struggling to negotiate their way through mud. Lilac muttered under her breath. She and Matt and Kerise had known that interference by HomeSec, directly or by proxy, was a strong possibility now that Matt had failed to communicate with the number given him on television. She had hoped for more time.

Silly rabbit...

She stepped into the church and shut the door behind her. The altar and richness of the cover, and the gold chalice, told her that this was a Roman Catholic chapel. Along the rude walls hung Stations of the Cross, and a statue of the Virgin Mary stood on a makeshift plinth of carved hardwood behind the pulpit. Off to one side, a priest in black turned around at her entry. He was black, and possibly had been trained and ordained from this very hamlet. He faced her squarely, a question on his face.

"Do you speak English?" Lilac asked.

He stepped forward. "You are American?" he said, his accent lightly French.

Her French was abysmal. "Listen, I need to find a girl named Veronique Ladama. Some men are coming for her. They are bad men."

He came to a stop before her, just out of reach. "If it is God's will, my child, they will take her. If it is His will, she will be safe."

Unable to credit what she had just heard, Lilac's jaw dropped. She stepped back. The words that were in her mind did not make it to her lips. Instead, she said, "Tell me where she is."

The priest shrugged. "It is mid-day. She will be tending

the gardens north of this village." His eyes flicked in that direction.

Unable to teleport there because she had no image to guide her, Lilac dashed from the chapel and ran faster than she had ever run in her life. The garden was there as advertised, and several children of various ages were weeding scraggly plants, under the supervision of three women. The youngest of the three was dressed well, and carried a cane, which she applied to keep the children working.

The sounds of the vehicles grew louder. Lilac called out, "Veronique Ladama?"

A thin girl of about ten slowly straightened from her labors and looked at her. She was attired in a rag of light brown cloth that served as a wrap-around skirt. Her hair was long and tangled, and streaks of dried blood marked the stripes she had been given by the cane.

Thunderclouds roiled in Lilac's mind. She wanted to kill someone.

She held out her arms and beckoned the girl forward. The woman with the cane started to object, and frowned, white showing all around her pupils. Lilac glanced back. Four men in fatigues stood at the edge of the garden. Two were white; the other two looked as if they were soldiers of the Senegalese army. Their rifles were aimed at her.

To transfer with the girl, Lilac required physical contact with her. Holding hands would suffice. But she could not reach the girl before the men opened fire. Of course, she had no way of knowing who they had come for. If for her, the girl might be safe. She raised her hands and turned to face them directly.

One of them men slung his rifle and began to thumb through some papers about the size of a passport. Finally he looked up and spoke to the man beside him. "She's one of the secondary targets of acquisition," he said, and looked at her for confirmation. "Your name?"

"Nuala Lowry," she answered.

She could transfer by herself, and no harm done. But they would settle for Veronique. Silently she swore, and dipped her head in a tiny nod. All right, then.

⸻

Washington, D.C.

Teague rode the bus all the way to the station and then back out to the park by the safe house. Almost two hours had passed since he had neutralized Al Rother. By this time, he was certain that Rother had been found, with the safe house and the surveillance now regarded as compromised. The last thing HomeSec would expect him to do was return to a known site. But with an All-Points issued on him now, he saw no other choice; if HomeSec had foreseen this maneuver, so be it.

The loss of Rother hurt. In his work, trust was a commodity, to be exchanged or abandoned as needed. Still, a part of Teague regretted the betrayal. He even understood Rother's reasons for it: you see to your own first. This Rother had done.

Teague selected a bench that was hidden from the safe house and studied his periphery. Several cars were parked along the four streets, none of them occupied. None possessed the flavor—or the aroma—of a government vehicle. Off to his left, a woman was playing with two young children, presumably her own. At one corner of the park, an old man in a gray overcoat sat tossing popcorn to pigeons. Teague sighed. He himself had used associates to create a harmless appearance. But what he saw at the moment did not arouse his suspicions.

He got up and moved around, constantly checking his surroundings. Eventually he made off in the direction of the tree where he had left Al Rother. Approaching, he slowed, quickly looking around before he focused on the body at the base of the trunk. Was Rother dead? Had he inadvertently killed him? Or was this a trap, with Rother baiting a sentimentality that he, Teague, did not possess? He hesitated; in the end, he had to know.

He knelt down beside Rother and felt for a pulse. It was there, strong and steady. At the contact, Rother groaned. His hand fluttered to the back of his head. Teague sat back on his heels.

"Idiot," he said softly.

188

"Wha you doin' 'ere?"

"Got nowhere else to go," said Teague, one eye on Rother and the other watching for danger. "I missed my ride. So they left you here?"

"After 'nother crack onna head." Rother sat up and leaned back against the tree. Gradually his eyes focused. "Something's happened," he said. "I don't know what, and I wasn't really in a position to ask. But they moved away as if they had been called to a much bigger problem."

"I was wondering...," Teague admitted.

Rother looked up at him. "So now what?"

Teague dared not ask Rother to trust him. In the business, that word all too often presaged betrayal—and Rother had betrayed him, which would increase his suspicion. Teague held some hope of rescue, if Kerise and Analou had enough influence over Matthew Porter. Not that he himself needed it. The project had reached a point where he, Teague, could expect his payment from Renaud for services rendered. And he still had a debt to collect.

He held out a hand to Rother, and helped him to his feet. "Do you want to live forever?" he said.

030

eastern Senegal

The man stuffed papers back into his shirt pocket. "The girl, too" he said, with a little gesture toward one of the Senegalese.

Fear widened the dark eyes of Veronique Yadama. She edged back a step, and glanced at the surrounding jungle, as if considering whether to flee. She was just four paces from Lilac. So close, yet still too far. Lilac bit at her lower lip in frustration. It would be so much simpler if she had physical contact with the girl. She closed her eyes and focused.

Scant seconds later, the man with the papers and the slung rifle cried out in agony. The back of his fatigue shirt was smoking, but it was the rifle barrel, now a blackened orange color that radiated light as well as heat, that caused the fabric to ignite. He screamed, and struggled out of the sling, and cast the weapon onto the ground. His three comrades were also agitated, and cast their glowing weapons into the mud.

While the men stared in shock and horror at the steam rising from the mud, Lilac reached for the girl, and knelt down in front of her. Quickly she said, "English?"

Veronique nodded while she stared at the stricken men.

"I am a friend of Matthew Porter," Lilac went on. "He sent me here. I have to ask you: do you wish to come with me to him? Or would you rather stay here?"

The girl frowned. "*Qui?* Who?"

"Matthew. Matthew Porter. You do know him, right?"

She shook her head.

"Omigod," whispered Lilac, and cursed. Somewhere along the line, Porter's donations had gone astray. That explained the girl's appearance. Didn't anyone bother to check? "Goddamn it," she said. She took the girl's hands, speaking with urgency now. "I can get you out of here, Veronique, but I need you to tell me that this is what you want."

"Y-yes. *Es-tu americaine?*"

That, Lilac understood. She stood up, still holding Veronique's hand. Several paces away, the men were recovering. One of them also carried a pistol in a black leather holster on his web belt. He was reaching for it now.

In the next moment, she and the girl were inside the church. Their abrupt appearance stunned the priest, who was inspecting the pews for the coming service. His mouth worked, but no sounds came out.

"The *Kinderheim* money and packages for Veronique," said Lilac. Acid bit the back of her throat, and accompanied her words. Her eyes surveyed the finery on the altar. "You kept the money for yourself."

"For God," said the priest. "Donations are for the Lord's work."

"The clothing, the food..." Dispirited, Lilac sighed. "The donations were *Kinderheim*'s work, for the children. You intercepted it. You stole it."

The priest seemed shocked by the accusation. "I do the work of the Lord, young woman."

"Yeah, I've seen photos of the Vatican." Again she exhaled, this time in a growl. The golden chalice caught her eye. A moment later, it was a glob of molten metal, seeping over the edge of the altar.

And in the next moment, Lilac and Veronique were gone, the horrified shriek of the priest fading to darkness.

⁂

Nicaragua interior

Soldiers were already present in the *lugarillo* when Matt, Kerise, and Manorema arrived at the stone and wood hut where Miguel Dario lived. The boy was astonished to see them materialize out of thin air. His mother fainted; his father crossed himself, and stepped forward as if to challenge them. Quickly Matt displayed empty hands. Outside, men were shouting in a dialect of Spanish that he could barely make out.

"*Paz, por favor,*" he said. After introducing himself and his companions, he hastened to give an abbreviated explanation for their visit. From the expression on the senior Dario's face, Matt was not certain how much the man comprehended. But he clearly understood the soldiers.

"They will harm the boy?" he asked.

Matt's lips tightened. "It's me they want," he said. "But they are searching for Miguel. You understand?"

Dario nodded vigorously, and led them to the back door. "This way."

"Quickly, Matt," said Kerise. "We're next."

A bullet ricocheted off the stone wall in the front room. An edge of panic made his ribs ache. Dimly he heard another shot, and at the same time the back of his head received a heavy blow that made all his inner lights go on. Despair cloaked his mind. He saw Kerise's face hovering above his. It morphed into Lilac's, and the world went dark.

Columbus, Ohio

Geneva Hartland stood by triumphantly while a road crew with jackhammers carved away the asphalt overlying the gasoline reservoir. Already an optical fiber had been inserted into the fill pipe and had confirmed Hartland's incredible and impossible assertion. The faces of the men around her bore expressions of shocked disbelief despite the proof of the fiber.

Doubtless, she thought, they were wondering just how the *hell* he had gotten *in* there. Besides herself, only Frank Church, standing next her pale and drawn, knew.

After communication had been established with the President, he was given a caution to retreat to a far corner of the reservoir. A man with a cutting torch removed a three-foot square from the metal top. A ladder was inserted into the reservoir, and a paramedic with an aid case and a long overcoat climbed down inside, accompanied by a Secret Service agent. The view through the optical fiber appeared on a monitor that only two other agents were allowed to watch.

After five minutes, the President's head appeared in the

opening. With the assistance of the Secret Service, he stumbled up and out. Hartland was not shocked by his overall appearance, but there was something wrong with his eyes. Presently it struck her that he had suffered severe psycho-emotional damage during his confinement. It was the equivalent of prolonged sensory deprivation. Someone, she thought, should notify the Vice-President, who would take over under the provisions of the 25th Amendment. Someone, but that was not her job. The DCI had determined that she should resume control of Echelon.

Brussels, Belgium

Langford and Sylvie sat in utter silence after watching the contents of the Renaud flash drive. He heard only the beating of his heart. Even his respiration made no sound. He pinched his arm to find out—only half in jest—whether he was still alive. A part of him wished he knew what Sylvie was thinking. The rest of him struggled to think of something to say.

It was Sylvie who broke the sound barrier. "It is that I believe him," she said, hushed. "It is that he can do this."

There was a different quality to her voice now, something that—despite a few manic moments—had not been present before. It sounded to Langford almost like hope. But hope for what?

"Do you suppose there are other flash drives?" he asked.

Sylvie nodded hesitantly. "It is that this is too important to entrust to one source," she answered. "The multiple sources not merely confirm the information, but induce the credibility." The tip of her index finger caressed the drive now resting on her lap. "He wants the Earth to know why."

"And he is safe," Langford put in. "He knows he cannot be stopped."

For several seconds Sylvie was silent. "I can stop him," she said quietly.

He stared at her. "How?"

"It is to use the key to backtrace the signal of the opening."

"And... you have done this. You know where he is."

"I have done this. I know where he is."

Washington, D.C.

"It's incredible," said Rother.

"But true."

They were sitting in a small café several blocks away from the safe house. The neighborhood, like much of Washington, D.C., was run-down and unsavory, but there were only two other patrons inside, both of them derelicts in shoddy overcoats, each nursing a mug of coffee. They were out of hearing range.

"Oh, I believe you," said Rother. He turned his half-empty second mug this way and that, using the bottom to trace designs in the condensation on the tablecloth. "What I don't understand is why you are not going."

"*Do* you want to go?"

"Yes. I mean, hell yes! But... Teague, *why?*"

Teague sat back, his face devoid of expression, of emotion, and Rother knew he had touched an exposed nerve. But Teague was not angry at the intrusion, or at Rother himself. It occurred to Rother that this was the first time he had seen Teague downcast.

"In some ways," said Teague, his voice heavy and weary, "it happened yesterday. It's still fresh. But it's been more than a quarter of a century now, and still it remains vivid." He drained his mug and set it down with deliberate care, as if he were avoiding the desire to shatter it against the table. His controlled anger made Rother shift in his seat.

"I owe them a response, Al," he said. "Think of it as me being wired this way. Their religion said it was not merely permissible, but a duty, to murder my wife and children. I am going to respond according to the precepts of my religion."

Suddenly he raised a hand. "Don't, Al. I can see it in your eyes. You talk to want me out of this. Just bet it le.

Go with them. Get out of here. It doesn't matter what happens here because you'll never return. None of them plan to return."

"What... what are you going to do?

"Something massive," Teague replied.

⁕

Northwest Brazil

Raw fear surged through Matt as he opened his eyes. Immediately a hand pressed firmly on his chest, holding him down.

"Shh." A female voice. "It's all right. You're okay. We're okay."

"Lilac?" His own voice sounded fuzzy. He opened his eyes to Kerise's face. It was Lilac's hand on his chest, more gently now as he recovered. He turned his head to see both Manorema and Miguel and...Veronique?

He sat up to a momentary dizziness, and touched fingertips to the back of his head. A gauze bandage had been taped there. Kerise steadied him. They were all six in her bedroom at the Indigo site—the adults on the bed, the children in chairs that had been brought in.

"I'll answer your question," she said. "Lilac made an inspired guess, thinking you and I might need help. She got us all out of there... obviously in time. I showed her my bedroom on my Palmetto... and here we are."

"Simple," he said. "And my head?"

"A chunk of adobe broke loose during the gunfire, and struck you." A worried look darkened her face. "Matt... just to be sure, would you transfer to the hallway outside?"

It took him a moment to find the image in his memory. A couple of seconds later, he stood in her doorway. Miguel cried out, and squirmed closer to Manorema.

Matt flashed a crooked smile. "Looks like you still need me," he told Kerise.

Now the look morphed to one of hurt. Lilac said, "That's unfair."

He entered, and flopped back down. "Sorry—"

"You should be," Lilac grated. "You are far more than

just a telekine, and *that's* what we both love you for. Look around you, dammit. There are two children here who adore you." In a softer voice, she added, "The third had no idea who you were."

That galvanized Matt. "*What?*"

"It seems the hamlet's priest, who was in a position to intercept the benefits from *Kinderheim*, did so," Kerise explained. Her eyes flicked to Veronique and back, as if warning him not to comment. "He spent the money on religious finery, and sold the clothes and food. She was in filthy rags when Lilac found her. The clothes she's wearing now came from us. Lilac went to a store and wasn't sure of the size of jeans she should wear...but I think she'll grow into them soon. And yes, now she knows who you are, and what you were trying to do for her."

"That priest," growled Matt. "I'll—"

"It's been done," Lilac said. She grinned wickedly. "There's an Inuit village in the northern Yukon that has very little contact with the outside world. I think he'll do well on a diet of whale blubber."

Matt laughed. "You didn't."

"Of course I did. Maybe I shouldn't have bothered. We're leaving all this behind, Matt. What do we care? Oh, it's not an easy decision to make. But we could spend our entire lives trying to... to..."

"Fix the system?" supplied Matt.

"Yeah. Good choice of words. Fix the system, and in the end, even if we had as much as a teensy effect, there would be more problems. Governments and societies seem to be hard-wired to create them. Maybe Indigo won't be any different, but at the very least it will give us the possibilities inherent in a fresh start."

Veronique got up at last to sit beside Matt, her eyes glowing with wonder. He slipped an arm around her shoulders and gave her a hug.

"The President?" he said.

"Is no longer in office," Kerise answered. "25th Amendment process. He was in no mental or emotional condition to resume office. At the moment, he's convalescing in a private ward in Johns Hopkins. The prognosis is... unfavorable. He hasn't reached the stage where he drools his pabulum, but he'll need some assisted living. None of this except the bit with the amendment has made or will make the news, of course. My Dad has... sources." She eyed him carefully. "Is that... enough for you?"

"I have my pound of flesh," he replied, and glanced at Veronique. "I am content."

"Shylock," muttered Lilac.

"There is one other problem," said Kerise. "We may have to depart early. I think we've been discovered."

031

Northwest Brazil

At the knock on his door, Simon-Louis Renaud looked up from his laptop to find, as expected, Kerise sweeping into the office like a whirlwind. She was wearing a white knit cotton top with a blue eagle embroidered on it, and a blue and black floral skirt long enough to cover her shoes. In that outfit, she reminded Renaud of her mother, and he had to close his eyes for a moment. When he opened them again, she was sprawled on an armchair, regarding him with soft gray eyes.

"Would you care for a drink?" he asked.

Kerise shook her head. "Do we know who it is?"

"We were aware of the attempt, of course. I authorized a team to neutralize it, but it seems the tables were turned."

"Langford," she said. "Beginner's luck."

"It would seem so." He got up and poured himself a brandy. "The lock has been opened by someone inside Interpol in Brussels. That can only be Sylvie Dubray. She now has my departing statement. The backtrace came to us here—my mistake." He sighed. "My hubris. I had thought the lock utterly secure. There is always someone more skilled."

Kerise frowned thoughtfully. "You, we, couldn't have known that Langford would make contact with Interpol. In fact," she sat up straight, "why would he have done? On what basis? That an unidentified individual gave him a timed flash drive. Do not open till Christmas?" She shook her head and thought back. "No, no, it has to be something else. Something... I did. He... was holding a Palmetto." She moaned. "And he got enough of my face to send it to an Interpol connection for facial recognition. *Merde!*"

"Do not blame yourself, Kerise."

"Whom, then?" She made a fist and bashed it against the top of her thigh. As abruptly as the outburst began, it ended, and her face was calm once more. Even the freckles were merry. "So why aren't they here?" she asked.

Renaud sat back down. "That did puzzle me, *c'est vrai*. With all the security services looking for me, you would think they would jump at the chance to confirm a lead like this. But perhaps it is not Interpol."

"I do not understand."

"Sylvie Dubray is distantly related to Lionel Dubray, a significant figure in the Resistance during World War 2. Her loyalty has not been known to be questioned, but perhaps in this instance, she has…"

"Another agenda?" suggested Kerise. "Can you get in touch with her?"

Renaud shook his head. "It would have to pass through the Interpol net."

"Why not send it back along the backtrace? If she is working on this on her own, it might not require clearance through Interpol. It would go directly to her computer."

Renaud smiled. "What is it the Americans say? That sounds like a plan? *Eh bien*. There remains then only the matter of the payment to Teague. He was sent by your Analou to Washington to see to a friend of his who had asked for help. I have no way of making contact with him, to tell him where his payment is located."

"I do not understand. This should be a simple transfer of funds."

"Ah, if it were but that simple."

Uh-oh, said Kerise's expression. "Tell me," she said.

He did. She did not like it.

⚓

Brussels, Belgium

Sylvie returned to the front room deep in thought. She almost stumbled over Langford's feet before she finally came to rest in an armchair, facing him. To him, she looked as if she had just walked into a stanchion she hadn't seen. Gradually her eyes came to focus on him. A smile toyed with the corners of her mouth.

"Bad news?" he asked.

A hesitation while she drew a breath. "I am not the

certain."

Langford bit at his lower lip. He had already come to accept her English syntax, but her statement now went beyond that. She was shaken. But she did not seem to be frightened. He started to get up from the sofa, but she stopped him with a raised hand.

"It is at you I wish to look," she said.

"Sylvie—"

"We have been pinged, Evan. They know we know. We have been invited." She paused for another breath, this one deeper. Under the loose white peasant blouse her thin shoulders trembled with effort. "It is that I wish to go," she said bravely. "I have thought this; I have given this the thought." Her hands fluttered. "Oh, I do not know how to say it."

"You have thought about this."

"Yes! *Oui!* B-but..."

A smile touched his tone. "And you are worried about what I will say."

"I do not want to... to... lose..."

"Sylvie, you have a job as a tech wizard. Isn't it your responsibility to pass on this information to Montclair? Yet you have not done so. Sylvie, in the same way, I have a job as a reporter. I have the scoop of a lifetime. Yet I have not yet begun to put words together."

She tilted her head to one side, one eyebrow raised. "What is the scoop?"

"It is a news story no other journalist has."

"Ah. And you have not made the story, *n'est-ce pas*? The report?"

"Perhaps they will have need of a historian as well as a tech wiz."

Her eyes widened. "Ah? What you say to me?"

"We go together."

She got up and dropped to her knees before him, her head resting against his chest. She was still trembling. He held her until she was still.

"*Biensûr,*" she whispered.

<hr>

Washington, D.C.

Kerise and Matt found Teague and Rother inside the safe house. There had been a moment when Teague, seeing them suddenly materialize in the light of the single candle, had his sidearm out and aimed before they stopped blinking. But he identified his targets and withheld fire. Rother, meanwhile, staggered and slumped against a wall.

"You'll get used to it," Teague told him. To Kerise, he added, "*Mon paiement?*"

"Teague, you can't do this," she said.

"He would send you, of course," he said bitterly. "He never meant to pay me."

Kerise's voice was as quiet as the house. "That's where you're wrong," she said. "The fact is, I do possess the information you want. I will pass it on to you. But first I will be heard."

"How—" gasped Rother, recovering.

"Magic," answered Matt. "Now be quiet."

"You have nothing to say to me that I want to hear, Kerise," said Teague. "It's over. I'm done. I've fulfilled my contract. Now, where is the Mirage?"

"You're going to murder at least two million people, and probably a lot more," she went on smoothly. For a moment her gaze touched his face. Then her shoulders fell. "*Mon Dieu!* Strafe the pilgrims during the *hajj*, and then nuke Mecca?"

"*They deserve it!*" he roared. His hands hacked at the air around him, as if seeking a target not yet visible."

A hard look came over her. "*Vraiment?* Oh, perhaps some do. Those who cheered, or fired rifles into the air in celebration, when the Towers went down. Those who gave tacit approval to the attacks, even if they had no connection to them. I agree. *D'accord.* But you are not the agent of their destruction, Teague. They will do that themselves, in their petty wars over who had the right to be caliph a millennium ago. But this, this is not you. I know you are angry, enraged, distraught. What human being wouldn't be? And you have killed often before. *Le mort n'est pas l'inconnu à toi.* It was part of your job. But what you mean to do is no part of your job."

He pointed a shaky hand at her. "Don't... don't you tell me I'm like them. They murdered my wife and my son. Don't you dare compare me with them, young woman!"

"I would never! The morality is in no way the same. Prey do not become predators by killing predators. They only stop being prey." Her voice softened. "But those on *hajj* are not predators. They *are* like you. Fathers, brothers, uncles. Wives, sisters, aunts. Women. Children. Children, Teague."

"And... and don't remind me that this will not bring Claire and Thomas back. It won't. I *know* that. God *damn* it, how well I know that."

"No, it won't. That cannot be done. You will not forget, nor will you forgive, and that is perhaps as it should be." She paused for a shuddering breath. "But close your eyes. See them—"

"Oh, God, don't."

"See them. They look at—"

"Don't," he moaned.

"Kerise," said Matt.

She glance at him sharply, a warning, and returned to Teague. "Look at you," she went on. "Would they—"

"Don't ask me that!"

Her voice became steel. "Would they want you to do this?"

His eyes red even in the dim light, he made a fist and took a step toward her. She stood very still. Another moan escaped him. Then he wailed, a million doves pining for lost loves, and smashed his fist into the wall. Plaster shattered, and lathes snapped. The impact made dust fall from the ceiling. He dropped to his knees there, and wept. His entire body quaked. Gradually he leaned forward, hugging himself, until his forehead touched the floor.

"Teague," whispered Rother.

Matt eased aside. "Go to him."

Hesitantly, Rother approached. Kerise backed away to join Matt. Her knees gave way, and she slumped against him. Her eyelids fluttered. He said nothing, but kissed her forehead.

She nodded against him. "It's time," she whispered. "It's done."

"What are you going to do?"

Resolution flowed into her, and she straightened. "What I was sent here to do," she said. "My job."

She stepped to Teague and waited for him to look up. His eyes were wet, his lips glistening. Rother, kneeling beside him, watched her with questioning eyes.

"There is a private hangar at the airport in Nice," she said. "The Mirage is fully fueled, and with auxiliary tanks. There is only enough fuel to get you there, plus half an hour or so—but that will not matter to you. The twenty-mike-mikes have ten thousand rounds. The nuclear missile is fixed to the wing. You will have to arm it before you fire." She glanced at Matt, and then back. "Thank you for all your help," she said, and bent to touch his arm. "So long, Teague." To Rother she added, "Your choice: us, or stay."

Neither man responded. Presently she drifted back to Matt. Their eyes met. "Let's go," she said. "Lilac will be waiting for us, as will the... our children."

"Wait," muttered Teague.

Northwest Brazil

"There's one thing I haven't figured out," said Langford. "Well, more than one, a lot more. But this: why August 27th?"

Renaud raised his tumbler in a silent toast, and took a sip of scotch. "That is the day the Parliament passed the seventy-five percent tax on the rich," he said. "That was the day I decided to leave. Kerise said, go where? In that very moment, I knew what I had to do. I spent the next five years putting it all together. She found the final piece."

"The paranormals."

"One paranormal in particular." His eyes took in Kerise and Matt and Lilac. "I still believe we would have solved—and will solve—the FTL problem. For centuries, for millennia, we have been a species that pushed against frontiers. We have abandoned that push into the possible, instead salting ourselves away like sardines, with more and more people and nowhere to go." He sighed. "*Eh bien.*

That is an argument for another time. We must leave while we still can, *M'sieur* Langford."

"Evan."

"And I am Sylvie."

"Of course. I agree with you, we ought to have a biographer, and another tech expert. Once we are in space, my files and my story, and the stories of everyone else involved, will be made available to you...Evan." He grinned. "Try not to get in our way."

"And the name 'Indigo,'" added Langford.

Kerise answered. "It is a color in the rainbow, in the spectrum, that only a few people are capable of seeing, even though it is right there in front of them."

She paused, looking at her father.

"See that everything is secured," he told her. "We'll rotate to simulate gravity as soon as we are in space. Personnel at necessary stations only; everyone else in quarters till we are free of Earth."

Her only response was a smile.

"*M'sieur* Lang—Evan, it seems the date you were given for broadcast was incorrect. Kerise will assist you in communicating with your headquarters, and with broadcasting the video I made, insofar as that will be allowed by Earth. Now, if you will excuse me, I have my own departure tasks to perform."

⚬

They walked the hallway, each alongside a *Kinderheim* child. Matt's thoughts gradually drifted from Veronique to what he and Lilac had to do. As he had explained to Renaud, mass and distance and even time had no meaning in telekinetics. All that was necessary, at least for Lilac and himself, were clear images of the object to be moved—in this case, the *Indigo*—and the location to which to move them. Tim*ing* was important: they had to make the transfer together. Imagery was also important: they had to envision the same destination. In practice this meant the same stellar photograph as a guide. For the first leg of the journey, the image they planned to use was a *Galileo* photograph of Jupiter taken from five million miles away. From that point in space, they would move the ship toward one of the planets photographed by the Habitable Exoplanet Imaging Mission. In the meantime...

"Do you want to be there when they make the broadcast?" asked Kerise, shattering his thoughts.

Matt shook his head. "We can watch it in the snack room. Let Langford and that French woman have their day in the sun."

"Sylvie Dubray. She's the only person who has ever gotten past Renaud tech security. Incidentally, you have a fan."

Veronique's adoring eyes remained fixed on him. She stumbled now and then against his boot, not watching where she was going.

"There was a time," said Matt, walking carefully, "when I was afraid this was all the good I would get to do. Now... now I don't quite know what I'm doing, only that I want to... to... you could help me finish this thought, you know. I need a good cliché now."

"Follow the path you're on?" suggested Lilac.

"Here you are," said Kerise.

"Yes. Here I am. I'm here. If those HabEx photos are accurate, we'll soon be there. Then... that's where I hit a wall, Kerise. I can't see what happens after that."

He felt Lilac's hand on his shoulder, and turned his head. Her other hand was on Kerise. "We'll find out together," she said. "How's that for a cliché?"

"Yeah," Matt said slowly. "But it all seems so Randian, what we're doing."

"With a difference," Kerise agreed. "Unlike the people in Galt's Gulch, we are not coming back, ever."

As they reached the snack room, speakers crackled. Langford's voice was first. Matt wondered how many stations and newspapers would carry the announcement, but in the end it wouldn't matter. He helped seat the children, and went with Lilac to the buffet, his eyes on the monitor in a corner of the room. It displayed Renaud's face now. He began to speak.

"People of Earth: my name is Simon-Louis Renaud. Until recently, I owned and operated Renaud Aeronautics in Lyon, France. I am speaking to you today for the very last time.

"It has become manifest that the people of Earth are not going to solve their problems or resolve their social ills. I am not speaking of wars, although too many contemporary conflicts seem interminable, particularly those in the Middle East. No, I am speaking of social conflicts. I need not enumerate all of them. A few examples suffice: the re-education camps in western China; the warlords of Africa and dictators in Latin America who deem it more important to gain power than to manage the development of their people and their resources; the failure of countries—and especially countries with coastlines—to address the *consequences* of global climate change as well as, and too often instead of, the *causes* of it; the ubiquitous and burgeoning bigotry and hatred of various social groups by other social groups; the destruction of Earth's environments—most blatantly in Brazil—to feed a population whose growth is raging out of control; the hatred of the rich by the poor, of the haves by the have-nots, as if it were somehow the fault of the wealthy that poverty exists.

"In fact, I had chosen August 27th to issue this statement—and to depart—because it is the anniversary of the vote of the French Parliament to tax the wealthy of France at the rate of 75%. However, circumstances have made it both possible and prudent to depart today. When that vote to rob the rich was held, I knew it was time to leave. But go where? The United States of America, which is along with Australia the last bastion of a few remaining freedoms, is bankrupt and wallowing in socialist mire. It cannot recover. *There is no other place to go.* The poor of the world, many fleeing from oppressive and tyrannical governments, as well as from wars, have inundated what is known as the West, which is to say Europe and North America. These hordes are wreaking havoc on economies, and it cannot help but worsen, until *all* nations are Third-World nations. With too many problems and not enough solutions, the societies of Earth will soon rupture—we see this process in effect daily—and inevitably those societies will collapse. It is too late to save you. The rich cannot save you; when their money is gone, forcibly distributed among you, what then will you do? I do not propose to remain and find out.

"Therefore: for the past five years now my daughter and I—with the help, I must say, of many other like-minded people, both rich and poor—have been constructing a craft to travel through space to other worlds. This craft, which we have christened *Indigo*, is capable of traveling far in excess of the velocity of light. It is now ready to depart. Even as you hear or read of this, we have already left you. For better or for worse, we will not return. I would like to wish you good luck, but the problems you have yourselves created and allowed to fester are well past the ability of fortune—or fortunes—to solve."

For a few seconds he paused, still gazing out at his unseen audience. When he spoke again, his tone was one of shaming.

"You could have had the stars," he concluded, and turned away.